Hearts
in the
Crosshairs

Center Point
Large Print

Hearts
in the
Crosshairs

Susan Page Davis

CENTER POINT PUBLISHING
THORNDIKE, MAINE

This Center Point Large Print edition
is published in the year 2009 by arrangement with
Harlequin Books S.A.

The text of this Large Print edition is unabridged.
In other aspects, this book may vary
from the original edition.
Printed in the United States of America.
Set in 16-point Times New Roman type.

ISBN: 978-1-60285-621-9

Library of Congress Cataloging-in-Publication Data

Davis, Susan Page.
   Hearts in the crosshairs / Susan Page Davis. -- Large print ed.
      p. cm.
   ISBN 978-1-60285-621-9 (library binding : alk. paper)
   1. Large type books. I. Title.
PS3604.A976H43 2009
   813'.6--dc22
2009027882

He has showed you, O man, what is good.
And what does the Lord require of you?
To act justly and to love mercy
and to walk humbly with your God.

—*Micah* 6:8

In loving memory of my mother,
Constance Wilson Page, who taught me
many things and is greatly missed.

Acknowledgments

My thanks to Steve McCausland, public information officer for the Maine State Police, and Sally Baughman, administrative assistant at the Blaine House. Any mistakes in this work are mine. I know you couldn't answer *all* of my many questions, and so I made some guesses and probably a few mistakes.

ONE

Governor Jillian Goff pulled on dark knit gloves as she walked across the lobby of the statehouse flanked by the president of the Maine Senate and two Executive Protection Unit officers. Another security officer opened the door, and she stepped out into the bright, cold January day. The sky overhead, between the Capitol and the state office building, shone a vivid blue. Several hundred people had crowded into the limited space. Jillian waved as she walked across the paving stones to the microphones, touched that so many had come out to see her just minutes after she took the oath of office.

She smiled and looked into the television camera with the red light. "I want to thank all of you, the people of Maine, for choosing me as your new governor. The past few months have been hectic, but they've been good preparation for what's ahead. Together we can bring Maine into a productive new era. I look forward to—"

A muffled *crack* made her freeze. Something zinged past her ear, and a small, sharp object struck her cheek.

Someone seized her shoulders from behind and shoved her down behind the bank of microphones.

"Steady, ma'am. Keep still until we secure the area."

She'd only been governor for fifteen minutes, and an officer from the EPU was holding her against the cold stone pavement before the door of the Capitol. Her right cheek stung. People shouted and scrambled about. A puff of white vapor formed in the air each time she let out a shallow breath. Her pulse thudded in her temples, and her knee hurt, folded beneath her on the freezing stone.

She turned her head, but that wasn't much better. Her cheekbone contacted with the icy pavement and she shivered. "W-what happened?"

"Shooter. Are you all right?"

"Yes."

Jillian swallowed hard. This morning, the chief officer of the Maine State Police, Colonel Gideon Smith, had urged her to wear a bulletproof vest beneath her coat during the press conference, and she had laughed at him. "When was the last time a Maine governor was attacked?"

"I take your safety seriously, ma'am," Smith had replied.

I should have listened to him.

Another man came and kneeled beside her.

"Are you all right, ma'am?"

"I think so." The cheek that was pressed against the stone still stung.

"We're going to help you up and get you inside.

We'll take you right up to your office. Do you understand?"

She nodded. She could hear the surge of the crowd and shouts in the distance.

"All right, then." The weight on her back lifted as the man who had hovered over her straightened, and she struggled to her knees.

"Quickly, now." The officers pulled her up and urged her toward the main door. A few photographers ran alongside and snapped pictures. Inside, a dozen people huddled against the walls, staring at her. Policemen surrounded her on all sides—plainclothesmen of the EPU, uniformed state troopers and Capitol security officers—but still she felt exposed. Anyone could have walked into the building before the press conference. She looked ahead, searching for things out of place, for people who didn't belong.

Six officers squeezed into the elevator with her. The rest headed for the stairs. So far, the emergency plan was functioning just as they'd laid it out to her a few weeks earlier.

"You're bleeding, ma'am," said one of the female detectives.

Jillian pulled off her gloves and touched her right cheek gingerly, then drew her hand away and looked at it. Her fingertips were stained with blood.

"I don't think it's serious."

"We'll have your doctor come look at it immediately," the tall detective on her other side said.

When they emerged on the floor above, Colonel Smith waited by the elevator, panting.

"Governor Goff! I'm so sorry." He took her elbow and guided her swiftly through the outer office and into the inner sanctum. Her private office. She'd only been in it a few times, during the last governor's term. Half a dozen EPU members and four uniformed troopers followed and took up positions at every door and window. Several more were ordered to stand guard in the outer office. The main door closed, and Smith locked it.

"Have a seat, ma'am. We'll get you out of here as quickly as possible, but not until we've secured the area."

"I understand." Jillian's chest tightened as she walked toward the huge walnut desk. At least her calf-length skirt and wool coat covered her trembling knees. She sank into the padded leather chair behind the desk and lowered her head into her hands. She winced as she touched her cheek again.

Smith held out a clean white handkerchief. "I'm sorry, Governor. We've called for your physician. She'll be here momentarily."

Jillian raised her chin. "I'm fine, Colonel. Just find out who did this."

• • •

Detective Dave Hutchins hurried to the Executive Protection Unit's afternoon briefing. The first attempt on a sitting Maine governor's life in many years promised to keep the unit busy.

"Were you there this morning?" Detective Penny Thurlow asked as he slid into a chair beside her.

"No," Dave said, "but I've seen it on TV at least ten times."

Penny nodded. "Me too. An assassination attempt on inauguration day. Unheard of."

Lieutenant Wilson, their immediate boss, briefed the officers. Heads turned as Colonel Gideon Smith, head of the Maine State Police, entered and took a seat near the door. Wilson wound down his spiel and nodded at Smith. "And now I'll let the colonel take the floor."

The officers sat up straighter as Smith walked to the lectern. "Men—and women—" he nodded deferentially to Penny and Stephanie Drake, the two female detectives in the unit "—I want to commend you and your colleagues for your exemplary performance today. Thanks to this unit, the governor of Maine is safe and sound at the Blaine House and will begin her official duties on schedule. It's up to you to keep the governor and her family safe, and to find out who made the attempt on her life. I don't need to tell you that this investigation is priority one for your unit. Any resources within my reach are at your disposal. Carry on."

The colonel turned on his heel and left the room. Dave glanced over at Penny. "Bet he wishes he was still doing field work, not pushing paper."

She nodded. "I'm on duty at the governor's office tomorrow. Can't wait."

Lieutenant Wilson resumed his place behind the lectern and opened a folder. "Assignments have been juggled due to this incident. We don't know yet who fired at the governor this morning. That means we've got to dig deeper into her past than any of her political opponents did during the last year, and that's pretty deep. We'll also reconstruct the shooting. We're reasonably sure this wasn't a sniping. The bullet came from the level of the crowd."

Dave leaned forward to listen, curious to know where he would fit into the aftermath.

"The Inaugural Ball has been canceled." A murmur spread across the room, and Wilson held up one hand. "It's unprecedented, but the governor's advisors were adamant. She should not go out in public until the situation is under control. So, those who drew duty for that event will have different assignments for tonight."

He named the officers who were currently on duty at the governor's mansion and assigned a new shift to relieve them. "The officers personally guarding Governor Goff will stagger their hours to preserve continuity. We don't want to leave any leeway for someone who's looking for a chance to get at the governor. We're also increasing manpower to guard her until further notice, so expect some overtime. We'll draw on state troopers for extra guards around the Blaine House as long as we feel it's warranted."

Dave drew duty investigating the shooting—his strong suit. But he envied the officers who would guard Jillian Goff. Not only did she carry herself with an air of sophisticated charm—class, Dave thought—but her file said she was intelligent and a gifted attorney. Since her husband's death, she'd thrown herself into the legislative process. He had to admire that.

He left the duty room, eager to get on with his assignment: interviewing Jillian's partners at the Waterville law firm where she had practiced before the election. Half a dozen other detectives would conduct interviews elsewhere, and their collective findings would give them a picture of the governor's relationships with the people closest to her.

The half-hour drive gave him time to think about the shooting. None of the officers on duty that morning had seen the gunman—the shooter had melted into the crowd.

How could it be that no one had seen the weapon or noticed the person who fired it? He clenched his hands on the steering wheel of his pickup. Easy. Every eye was on the glamorous new governor. The shooter had done the deed— not well, or he would have hit Jillian—and then stood his ground as part of the appalled audience. When the people panicked and fell back, away from the Capitol's public entrance, the person who wielded the gun went with them.

The shooter must have eased toward the fringe of the crowd. As soon as the ranks broke, he'd walked away to a vehicle parked on a side street or maybe down on State Street. Not in the Capitol complex parking lots, and not in the state employees' garage half a block up the street. Officers had secured those areas quickly and taken names and license plate numbers of everyone who left after the shooting. The massive job had taken hours, and a lot of people were unhappy about the delays.

Dave pulled into the parking lot at the office of Dandridge, Scribner, Harris & Goff. The partners were expecting him. They introduced themselves and took him into a conference room with a long, polished table.

"Terrible thing," said Martin Dandridge, the gray-haired senior partner. He offered Dave coffee, which he declined.

Margaret Harris, golden-haired and tanned, smiled at him, but the smile wavered. "When will the police know who did this?"

"We're doing everything we can." Dave studied her face. "I understand the governor's late husband, Brendon Goff, was also a member of this firm."

"Yes." Ms. Harris's mouth skewed into a grimace. "It was awful when Brendon died. He and Jillian met in law school. After a few years working with public prosecutors, they applied here together, and we brought them into the firm at the same time. Brilliant young couple."

"They were with us for five years or so before Brendon decided to run for Senate," Dandridge said. He shook his head. "Such a pity. If I'd known he was going to get himself killed, I'd have advised him to give up skiing. But he loved it. And you never know, do you? You just never know."

The other partners murmured their assent.

Dave cleared his throat. "So Jillian stepped into his seat in the Senate and then won reelection."

"Correct," said Dandridge. "And now our shining junior partner is governor of Maine. I can hardly believe it."

The third partner, Jon Scribner, leaned forward. "We took this morning off to go to Augusta and see her sworn in."

"So you were all there?" Dave looked around at the three of them.

Margaret nodded. "We closed the office for

the day. We only came in this afternoon because you called. Poor Jillian." She shook her head. "I tried to call her a couple of hours ago, but they wouldn't put my call through."

"The governor is under very close guard," Dave said.

"Well, that's good, I suppose."

Dave eyed them keenly. All had been at the scene of the shooting. And all knew Jillian well. How well? Well enough to want her dead?

TWO

Jillian ate dinner in the family dining room with her mother and her personal assistant, Naomi Plante. The guards outnumbered the diners, which she found disconcerting. Her mother, however, chattered on uninhibited as the staff served their meal.

Jillian realized she would have to get used to being waited on. She'd lived alone since Brendon died, eating a majority of her meals out of the microwave, so the hovering domestic staff put her a little on edge. Once the meal was over, she could retire to her private rooms with her mother, away from the watchful eyes. But even then, the security guards and staff would be only steps away.

She had hardly eaten all day, and she found the food delicious. Menu planning was one of the duties she had decided to delegate to her assistant. Sometime soon she'd have to talk to Naomi about meals, but right now, other thoughts occupied her.

Her mother might think she could distract her by talking about the décor, the food and the next week's schedule, but Jillian's mind kept skipping back to the shooting. Who wanted to kill her?

Every time she recalled the morning's events, her bewilderment morphed into anger. She took a deep breath and focused on her mother.

"It's such a pity they canceled your ball."

"Oh, I know," Naomi said quickly. "You bought such a beautiful dress, Mrs. Clark." She turned to Jillian. "And your gown! Will you ever wear it?"

Jillian shrugged. "There'll be another event." She chuckled. "I never was much of a dancer, anyway."

"Oh, but I *love* to dance," Naomi protested.

Jillian did feel a bit of regret for her mother's sake and Naomi's. Both had talked about the ball for weeks. Naomi bought her gown the day after election day, as soon as the ball was a sure thing. So much for the sure thing. It would have been the most prestigious event of Naomi's life, Jillian realized. Her mother's desolation, however, seemed more a cover for her anxiety about Jillian's welfare.

"Well, I'm glad they're looking after you," Vera said. "If that means no ball for you, then I guess we just stay home and turn into pumpkins. But it's such a waste. So many people booked rooms in town and bought special clothes. And all that food!"

"That's true," Jillian said. "I wish I could do something about that. I suggested a brief appearance, but the police said getting me there for a

18

few minutes would be as risky as a full evening out, and the organizers felt they should cancel it outright."

Her mother's shoulders drooped. "I do hope they can keep you safe, Jillian."

"They're trained for that, Mom."

They lingered over dessert and coffee without mentioning her narrow escape again. The lead officer on duty entered the dining room and approached her.

"Ma'am, Detective David Hutchins is here. He's one of the chief investigators of the incident. Would you like to see him now?"

"Certainly." Jillian pushed back her chair. "Show him into my private office upstairs, please." She wondered if that was the proper place for an interview with a police officer. Maybe she should take him into one of the public rooms across the hall—the sunroom or James G. Blaine's old study, for instance. But the windows in those rooms fronted on Capitol Street.

Even inside the well-guarded house, she felt vulnerable. This morning's incident had shaken her more than she'd admitted to anyone.

"Jillian," her mother called.

She looked back. "I won't be long, Mom. You and Naomi relax and make yourselves at home." She smiled at the irony of that. She was slowly absorbing the reality of living in this fabulous house. "I'll find you upstairs in a few minutes. Maybe the . . . family living room?"

The layout was still strange, and she had much to learn. She followed the hallway to the private stairs near the back of the house.

Finally, I'm alone for three seconds.

She heard muted steps behind her and shot a glance over her shoulder. One of the plainclothes officers of the EPU was only a couple of paces behind her.

At the top of the stairs, she caught a glimpse of a tall, dark-haired man entering her office. Another officer took up a post to one side of the doorway.

"Detective Hutchins is waiting for you, ma'am. We'll be right here if you need anything."

She tried to glance unobtrusively at his name tag. A. BROWNE.

"Thank you, Andrew." She hesitated and decided to be up-front. She hadn't mastered all the officers' and staff's names yet, but they were in this for four years. "It is Andrew, isn't it?"

"Yes, ma'am." He smiled and nodded as though she were a precocious child.

"Thank you." She ducked inside the office and closed the door behind her. For an instant, she lingered with her hand on the knob, facing the door. She'd known privacy would elude her after the inauguration, but she hadn't imagined how claustrophobic she would feel. She pulled in a deep breath, squared her shoulders, and turned.

"Good evening, Governor. I'm sorry to disturb you. Lieutenant Wilson asked me to update you before it got too late in the evening. I understand you have guests, and I won't keep you long."

She stood still, trying to assimilate her impressions. The smile seemed genuine. Something about it reminded her of Brendon, though the detective looked nothing like her late husband. Taller, a little sturdier. Less studious looking. More outdoorsy.

How long had she been staring? She stepped forward, extending her hand. "I'm delighted to meet you, Detective . . ." His warm fingers closed on her hand. She halted and looked in vain for a name tag. "I'm sorry, but your name slips my mind. I haven't James G. Blaine's talent for recalling them, I'm afraid. It didn't come with the house though he was famous for it."

He chuckled and released her hand. "Dave Hutchins. I'm pleased to be part of the unit looking out for you, ma'am."

"Oh, please. Let's not be 'ma'am' and 'sir.' I've had about all the formality I can stand for one day." She avoided the desk and sat down in one of the comfortable leather chairs before it, indicating with a wave of the hand that he should take the other.

He sat, and his long legs folded with athletic grace. His suit wasn't expensive, but he wore it well. He cocked his head slightly to one side, studying her. "Well, then, if you don't mind, please call me Dave."

She smiled. "Terrific. And you may call me—"

"Governor," he said gravely.

Not what she'd hoped for, but did she really expect the officers to call her Jillian? Of course not. It wasn't proper protocol. If she weren't so tired, she never would have entertained the idea. She put her hand up to her cheek. The small bandage below the corner of her right eye was her combat ribbon. She'd survived Day One.

"Are you all right?" Dave sat forward, his brow creased and his eyes sober. "Maybe I should come back tomorrow."

"No, I'm fine. It doesn't hurt, really." She managed a small smile. "The doctor said I should retire early, but not at seven-thirty. I'd like to know how the investigation is going."

"We're just starting, but we covered a lot of ground today. Our officers questioned witnesses and we searched the area where the press conference was held."

"Did you find anything?"

"The initial investigators did find a slug at the crime scene. It's somewhat distorted because it hit the stonework on the statehouse, but it could have been worse. It was a copper-jacketed bullet, probably from a nine-millimeter handgun. The bullet's in bad shape, but our ballistics team will do what they can."

"Do we know anything about the gunman?"

"Not specifically, but we have a rough estimate of where he or she probably stood."

She touched her cheek again. "The bullet chipped the granite wall beside me. They say that's what hit me—a piece of stone."

"Right. I believe you've stated that you heard the shot."

"Yes. It wasn't terribly loud, but it startled me. The officers pushed me to the ground." She shook her head, preferring not to remember those moments. "What else do we know?"

"We've approximated the angle from which the gun was fired."

"You followed the trajectory back from where the bullet hit the stonework?"

He smiled. "Exactly."

"And he wasn't on a rooftop somewhere."

"No. We're studying pictures of the crowd, trying to pinpoint him. But of course, most of the submitted photos and videotapes show you, not the audience."

She grimaced, wishing anew that she could perform her job without the requisite fame. She had plans for Maine, not so much for herself. Perhaps someone wanted to stop her from fulfilling her campaign promises.

"It sounds as though your unit is doing all the right things."

"I also drove to Waterville this afternoon

and spoke to your law partners."

"Oh." She sat back in the chair. "They were all here this morning."

"Yes. I talked to them about their impressions. They're intelligent people who are used to reading character, and they were only a few yards from you when it happened."

"You're not . . . looking at them as suspects, are you?" At once she knew the answer. "Of course you are. You have to."

He nodded reluctantly. "We can't rule out anyone yet. But I will tell you, they're not my top picks for this. They weren't standing near where the shot originated."

"Glad to hear it." She studied him, weighing where to file Dave Hutchins in her memory bank. She wouldn't forget the name again, or the serious brown eyes that could leap with laughter in an instant. Fine lines at the corners of his eyes spoke of fatigue, not just from today, but many days. His five o'clock shadow didn't lessen his attractiveness.

She realized he was sizing her up, too. Clearly he was good at his job.

The decision came quickly. She could count on him. File under *dependable,* but cross reference under . . . intriguing.

"The doctor said your wound is superficial," he said.

"It won't slow me down. I'll probably lose the

bandage tomorrow. I intend to present a strong image to the public."

"Good. In terms of proceeding with the investigation, I'll be looking into the background of anyone who may hold a grudge against you— perhaps someone you dealt with while you were in private practice, or during your stint as a public prosecutor."

"I suppose you're right. It all seems implausible, and yet . . ."

He smiled in sympathy, but continued. "We'll also look at political opponents. Will you jot down a list of names for me? Anyone you've crossed swords with in the past."

She shook her head. "I can't think of anyone who would want me dead. Not even Peter Harrison."

Dave's eyebrows rose. "You defeated him in the election. He wanted to be governor as badly as you did."

"Possibly more."

"But you don't think he'd lash out at you?"

"He was there with the VIPs when it happened. He was practically next to me."

"I know." Dave cleared his throat. "Governor, we've got to consider the likelihood that this was a hired hit."

She let that sink in. "A planned assassination? Aren't these things usually carried out by half-crazy whack jobs outside the political sphere?"

"Sometimes."

"Some kid could have the misguided impression that knocking off the new governor would impress his girlfriend."

Dave looked directly into her eyes, and her heart stuttered for a moment. "We can't discount any theories yet."

"But you think it was intentional, not a kook who doesn't realize what he's doing."

"I aim to find out, Governor. I promise you, I will do everything in my power to get to the bottom of this so that you can do your job in peace."

He smiled at her again, and she knew she'd sleep slightly better tonight, knowing that Dave Hutchins was looking out for her.

They left the office a few minutes later, after Jillian had given him a few names to start with— mostly criminals she had helped send to prison. Dave could easily check their statuses on his computer.

When they entered the hall, Andrew Browne stepped forward.

"Governor, Miss Plante and your mother are waiting for you in the family living room. However, a crowd of reporters has gathered outside. We've pulled all the drapes on this level, but you should be cautious about going near the windows. There's a small sitting room on the other side of the hall where—"

"I'll get my coat," she said. "Can I go out the door near the study?"

"Uh, ma'am—" Andrew shot Dave a glance and followed her down the hall. "You can't go outside, Governor."

"But the reporters need a sound bite. I saw the early news reports. Your spokesman's assurances that I wasn't seriously injured sounded almost too glib. I'd like to show them that I'm ready to face whatever comes my way." She pulled the bandage off her cheek in one quick jerk. "Seeing me hale and hearty will be worth a thousand speeches from aides."

"Governor." Dave caught up with her at the top of the stairs and touched her arm before he realized what he was doing. A no-no where protocol was concerned, but this could devolve into an emergency fast, and he needed to get her attention. "Jillian."

She stopped at the head of the stairs and turned slowly.

"I'm sorry," he said quickly. "I know you're determined to put the best spin on this, and I admire you for that. You're angry. You don't want to give the shooter the satisfaction of making you keep your head down."

"That's exactly how I feel." Her eyes gleamed as she looked up at him, and she caught her breath in a bitter chuckle.

He wished he could offer her more comfort, but words were the only solace he could give. "It's too dangerous. You could be playing into an assassin's hands by showing yourself so soon." She wavered. Her gaze darted to the stairs and back to him. "Please, Governor. You've got to let us do our job. Let the Public Safety Department's spokesman update the press again. I'll give him any message you want relayed to the public."

She pressed her lips together. He could sense her courage warring with her common sense. "Tell them . . . tell them I'll be in my office in the Capitol at 8:00 a.m., eager to put in my first full day as governor of Maine."

"Yes, ma'am." Dave jogged down the stairs, leaving her under Andrew's watchful eye. Andrew should be able to persuade her to join her mother now.

He called the department's official spokesman with her message and waited in the reception room downstairs until he saw Mark Payson's car pull into the yard. The spokesman got out and walked toward the reporters with his hands raised.

As Dave left the mansion and walked quickly toward the gate, he cased the crowd. It was up to him and a handful of others to catch the gunman before he could strike again. The clues were sparse, and so far the witnesses had given them nothing. Jillian had a full schedule for the next week. How could the EPU keep the governor safe if she made herself so accessible? Suddenly Dave felt inadequate for the job. It would take an army to keep the beautiful Jillian Goff alive.

THREE

Dave took a deep breath as he stepped through the family entrance at the Blaine House two days later. He'd always felt nervous coming into the governor's mansion. In the past, just the thought of meeting the state's chief executive set the adrenaline flowing. Knowing he had to get everything right the first time. Realizing he'd be scrutinized by the governor, his family and his staff every moment he was in the house.

By now he should have enough experience and confidence to stay calm when reporting to the governor. But his pulse cranked up several notches as he strode down the hallway, and he knew exactly why.

The anticipation of seeing Jillian. How had she held up under the strain of the last two days?

Yesterday, Lieutenant Wilson had updated her on the unit's investigation, but today he'd given Dave the assignment as an ongoing duty. He would see her frequently to report their progress.

He sent up a quick prayer for wisdom in fulfilling his responsibility. Detective Stephanie Drake met him in the doorway to the sunroom.

"Hi, Dave. The governor just returned from the

Capitol, but she'd like your update before she eats dinner. She asked me to send you upstairs to her private office, and she'll see you in about five minutes."

"Great. Thanks." He climbed the stairs. No one was posted at the doorway to her office this evening, but farther down the hall, a guard stood watch between him and the rest of the family quarters.

He entered Jillian's office and went to the window, which looked down on the yard that fronted on Capitol Street, across from the state-house. Dave pushed aside the curtain. He'd always thought the office would be more secure if it faced the backyard.

He caught the sound of soft footsteps muffled by the thick carpet and let the curtain fall. An older woman crossed the threshold, carrying a small tray that bore a steaming coffee mug and a square of cake on a china plate.

"Officer Hutchins?" Her skin wrinkled at the corners of her mouth as she smiled and held out her offering. She wore a matching skirt suit of thick, woven material, and her hair was neatly styled. She might have been an administrative assistant or a journalist, but the glint in her blue eyes reminded him of the face that had occupied his thoughts for the last two days.

"I'm Jillian's mother, Vera Clark."

"I'm pleased to meet you, Mrs. Clark." He

31

stepped toward her quickly and reached for the tray. "Is this for me?"

"Yes. Jillian was just about to join you, when she received an important phone call. She asked me to tell you she'd be along in a few minutes. I didn't think a cup of coffee could hurt a policeman who's been working hard all day."

Dave grinned. "Thanks very much."

Free of her burden, Vera lifted her left hand to her throat and fingered the bright red and white beads of her necklace. "Would you like cream and sugar?"

"No, black is fine, thanks." He hesitated. She still stood there, watching him with some sort of expectation. "Uh . . . would you like to sit down?"

"Thank you." She wasted no time in claiming one of the leather chairs. "That's blueberry cake. I baked it this morning and brought it along, but Jillian will only eat a sliver, to please me. She's very strict about carbohydrates."

"You made this cake?"

"Yes, with blueberries from the freezer. We picked them last summer."

Dave sank into the chair opposite her and picked up the fork, so as not to insult her. Beneath the streusel topping, the cake was bursting with plump blueberries. Just looking at it made his mouth water. He set the tray on the edge of Jillian's huge desk and took a forkful.

Vera watched him, her shoulders tense, her eyes questioning.

He nodded as he chewed and swallowed. "Delicious."

She exhaled and sat back. "Thank you. So what are you doing to protect Jillian?"

He blinked and reached for the coffee mug. "I'm involved in the investigation of the shooting, ma'am."

"And what have you got?"

He sipped the brew carefully and set the mug down. "Actually, I'm not allowed to discuss that with anyone outside my department. Except the governor, of course."

"Oh, of course." She tugged at the beads and looked away.

Dave realized her real mission was not to deliver a message or coddle a hardworking officer. She had come to worm some information out of him. He studied her for a moment. Mid-fifties, discreet makeup. She kept her nails short but well manicured. She was frightened for Jillian's safety.

"You're worried about your daughter," he said.

Vera leaned toward him, her hands clasped in her lap. "She's on edge over this shooting business. We all are. I thought the Executive Protection Unit would keep her safe."

"We're doing our best, Mrs. Clark."

Her eyes sparked for a moment. "Well, it's not good enough. Jillian was nearly killed Wednesday."

"Yes, ma'am. I know."

She sighed and shook her head. "I thought from the start that it was crazy to let her speak to the press outside like that."

"Well . . ." Dave lifted his shoulders and let them drop again. "It's tradition for the governor to make public appearances, and to give a press conference immediately after the swearing in. We've always been careful, and in the past, everything has been fine."

"This isn't the past. This is now, and she's my daughter." Vera's eyes narrowed and her jaw took on an unexpected firmness. "Officer Hutchins, if your unit doesn't keep my daughter safe, you'll have to answer to me."

Jillian paused in the doorway to her office. Her mother sat on the edge of her chair, glaring at Detective Hutchins, who gazed back rather sheepishly.

She glanced at Stephanie Drake, who stood guard outside the door. Stephanie quirked her eyebrows slightly, but said nothing.

Jillian leaned toward her and whispered, "What's going on?"

"Your mother's giving Dave Hutchins what for." Stephanie's barely suppressed smile quickly disappeared and she straightened her shoulders and looked forward.

Jillian pulled in a deep breath and walked into her office.

Dave said to her mother, "I assure you, ma'am, the governor has the best possible—" He noticed Jillian and leaped to his feet, jostling a tray of dishes on the edge of her desk.

She extended her hand and smiled. "Dave. It's good to see you again. I appreciate your stopping by to brief me. I hope it's not keeping you away from a family dinner."

His lips curved in a tight smile. "It's just me, ma'am. No problem."

Jillian wished she had the freedom to invite him to join her family dinner, but that wouldn't go over well in the upper echelon of Maine politics, she was sure.

The words "It's just me" echoed in her head. Was he single?

She caught herself and turned to her mother, trying to get her focus back.

"Mom, thanks for giving Detective Hutchins my message. I'll be with you and Naomi in half an hour."

"I hope I'm not delaying *your* dinner," Dave said.

"Oh, no." Vera chuckled as she stood. "They serve it too late here, anyway. Jillian, you should speak to that housekeeper about moving your supper up an hour."

Jillian managed to keep a smile on her face. "If you and Naomi would like an appetizer while you wait, feel free to ask the kitchen staff."

Vera sniffed and walked toward the doorway, but turned back. "Oh, Officer, you haven't finished your cake." She threw a meaningful look at Jillian. "*He* likes my blueberry cake."

"It's fantastic," Dave said.

"By all means, feel free to finish it while we talk," Jillian told him.

He glanced at her mother. "Thank you again, Mrs. Clark."

"You're welcome. I expect we'll see each other again."

At last she was out the door, and Jillian closed it gently. "I'm sorry."

"Your mother obviously cares about you."

"Yes." Almost too much sometimes, Jillian thought. She slipped past Dave and sat down in the chair her mother had occupied. "I do hope she didn't pester you too badly."

He grinned. "I can take it."

Her heart fluttered. Again he reminded her of Brendon—the carefree exterior that covered a more pensive attitude. She had to stop staring into his alert brown eyes. Next she would be sighing over her protector. Wasn't that a classic reaction from a woman in danger? She'd have to be careful to maintain protocol, despite his charming personality and striking features.

"Please have a seat, Dave. Would you like fresh coffee?"

"No, I'm fine, thanks. Will your mother be staying here with you?"

"She prefers her own home in Belgrade. It's more private, and it's close enough for her to see me whenever she wants. But I think I'll ask her to spend a week or so here while I get settled in my routine."

"Sounds like a good idea," Dave said.

"Even with the staff, one person alone could rattle around in this big old house."

She realized she'd just told Dave she found the Blaine House lonely, and quickly changed the subject. "So, are you any closer to catching the shooter?"

"We have some leads." Dave picked up a leather portfolio from beside his chair. As he reviewed it, she studied his profile. Not bad at all. Again she caught herself. She hadn't considered a romantic relationship since Brendon died, and she refused to think about one now. Even if she did, it couldn't be with someone from her security unit. She knew how to stick to business, and she would, even in her thoughts. Period.

He looked up and smiled. "I wish I could tell you we have a viable suspect, but we don't. Not yet. We have several avenues we're following, and you can be sure we're being extravigilant regarding your security."

Reaching up to her cheek, she fingered the scrape that was now almost invisible. "Can you be more specific about the leads you have?"

"Of course. I brought a few pictures for you to look at."

"Pictures?" She edged her chair closer to his.

"These were taken on Wednesday during your press conference. Some are stills from news crews' video footage. The others were submitted by newspaper photographers and people who took snapshots."

He passed the portfolio to her. Jillian looked down at the pictures arranged in plastic sleeves. Most were of her and the dignitaries who had stood near her that day: the previous governor and his wife, the state's congressional representatives, the senior members of the Maine legislature.

She flipped the page over. The next few were crowd shots, and she raised the portfolio, studying the sea of faces. "This one shows a group of volunteers who helped with the campaign. And these are my law partners." She glanced over the last few photos and handed the folder back to him. "So who are you looking at?"

"Well, the man you defeated, of course."

"Peter Harrison."

"Yes, and his staff."

"They wouldn't stoop so low."

"Are you sure?"

She shrugged. Politics was a tricky game, even

in a small state, and she'd overcome her naiveté long ago. But still.

"Peter and I are polar opposites on the energy issue, and he's quite passionate about it, but I don't think . . . No, I don't. Who else?"

He took a small notebook from his inside jacket pocket and consulted it. "How about Arthur Leeman?"

"He wasn't happy when I prosecuted him, but then I suspect he's never happy. He killed his wife and her sister. He's still in prison, isn't he?"

"Yes, but—"

"You think it was a hired hit."

"We can't rule it out. What about Robert Vincent?"

She thought back to the high-profile trial that preceded the embezzler's all-too-short incarceration. "I don't know. Maybe."

"So far, there's nothing definite on any of the people you helped convict," he said. "But we're also looking at a couple of men you defended in private practice. Defendants who lose their cases sometimes harbor resentment toward the attorneys who represented them."

She inhaled slowly, knowing he was right. Two cases came immediately to mind. In both instances, she knew she'd defended a guilty man. "Are you looking at Roderick Tanger?"

Dave nodded. "I sure am. And does the name Gerald Francis ring a bell?"

"Yes. Check them both." She shivered. Most of the time, she'd loved being an attorney, but there were days that still haunted her. "How will I know what you've found out?"

"I'll report to you at least once a week. More often if you'd like."

She looked down at her hands. A week seemed terribly long to go without an update on the search for a man who wanted her dead. She turned her plain gold wedding ring back and forth a few times, then raised her gaze to his.

"I suppose every day is too often?"

"Not if that's what you want."

She sighed and tried to reconcile her fear with her love of efficiency. "I probably don't need it that often, unless you have a breakthrough I should know about."

The lines of his mouth were straight and sober, though his eyes still radiated sympathy. "I don't want to intrude on your schedule, but if you'd like frequent updates, I'm open to that. I can meet with you as often as you want."

"Thank you." She hated the tremor in her voice. If Brendon were here, he'd know exactly what to do, and how often to ask the EPU to brief them. But if Brendon were alive, he would probably be governor, not Jillian. And he certainly wouldn't feel vulnerable and insecure right now. She straightened her shoulders. "Let's meet twice a week. Tuesday and Friday."

"Sure. Is this time good for you? I could come to your office in the statehouse earlier in the day, if you'd prefer it."

Jillian shook her head. "I'd rather meet here, if you don't mind. It's more private. Of course . . ." She looked up at him, suddenly aware that she might be inconveniencing him. "I don't want to prolong your workday. If it's easier for you—"

"Six o'clock will be fine, Governor. Whatever suits you best. And of course, we'll notify you immediately if something important comes up."

She nodded slowly. "Thank you. Dave—" She stopped and looked away. It seemed wrong, all of a sudden, for her to call him by his first name. "I'm sorry. Detective."

"Please. *Dave.* I'm comfortable with that if you are."

"All right." She inhaled in an effort to compose herself. He'd told her twice now, so she would use his given name and not feel guilty. "It's good to have someone who's not steeped in politics to discuss this with. Everyone at the statehouse is talking about it. They all have their theories as to who wants me dead."

"Who do they suggest?" he asked.

Her laugh came out higher pitched than normal. "Oh, lobbyists, criminals I prosecuted, someone even suggested a jilted boyfriend from my past. But I don't have any of those."

"Not a one?"

41

"Brendon was my first and only love." She swallowed the lump in her throat. "Genuine love, I mean."

Dave's gentle smile drew another blush from her.

"That's nice," he said softly. "But there could be an unbalanced man out there who imagines himself in love with you. Have you ever had anyone follow you? Maybe even while you were married, or when you were dating Brendon?"

She tried to ease the eerie feeling away by smoothing down a wrinkle in her skirt. "A stalker? I don't think so."

"Good. We think it's more likely someone with a professional grudge—either political or legal."

Which could encompass hundreds of people. The field of suspects was wide open. Some people would think it was hopeless, but Jillian didn't believe that. She'd never believed, as many people did, that the events of life were random. But would Dave understand that? She hesitated to mention it, but he needed to understand her mindset if he hoped to protect her.

"Dave, there's one thing you should know about me."

"What's that?" He watched her closely, and she suddenly felt that his interest went deeper than just a professional curiosity. She pushed the thought away.

"I believe in God. If there is someone out there who wants to kill me, he won't succeed unless God lets him. And if my assassination is part of God's plan, then there's nothing you and the whole of the Maine State Police can do to prevent it."

Their gazes locked for a long moment, and at last he broke the silence.

"I understand."

She relaxed, sinking back against the leather padding. "Do you? You don't think I'm too fatalistic?"

"Not at all."

"Some people do, so I've . . . I've stopped trying to explain it to them."

His eyes spilled compassion, and she knew she'd found an ally.

"Can you consider me a partner in solving this case?" she asked. "I want to be more than a spectator, and certainly more than the victim."

"Of course." He stood and extended his hand to her. She took it, enjoying the warmth of his strong grasp.

"Thank you again for coming. I'll see you Tuesday evening," she said.

"I'll look forward to it, and I'll call your office if anything comes up before then."

She watched him leave. His dark hair was cropped quite short in the back—shorter than Brendon's preferred style. It suited him very well. He turned at the door and nodded with a quick smile.

"Good night," she said.

If she were anyone but the governor . . . But she was the governor.

FOUR

A week later, Dave drove back to the office half an hour before his Friday meeting with Jillian. He just had time to shave in the men's room before heading over to the Blaine House. He wished he had better news for her. The EPU's lack of progress on the shooting case would soon become an embarrassment.

He'd effectively ruled out her former law partners and most of her Senate colleagues. The unit's list of people to check up on still included more than a hundred names, and the possibility remained that the shooter was an unknown who hadn't even hit their radar yet.

He hung his down jacket in his locker and took out his electric razor. A minute later, Carl Millbridge, an EPU detective with ten years' seniority over Dave, came in and trudged to his locker. Carl never saw things eye to eye with Dave, but they usually gave each other a wide berth and went on with their duties effectively ignoring each other.

"Howdy, Carl," Dave said over the buzz of his razor.

Carl glanced at him. "Got a date?"

"Not exactly." Dave suddenly felt self-conscious

about shaving for his meeting with the governor. "I'm getting together with some buddies from my old Marine unit." It was actually the truth. Two of the men who had served under Dave in Iraq would meet him at the Chinese buffet in a couple of hours. Let Carl think that was the reason for his careful grooming—though he'd never shave twice in one day for those guys. Dave shut off the razor and blew the whiskers from the blades.

"You making any headway on the inauguration day shooting?" Carl asked.

"Some. Not much."

Carl nodded. "Same here. Who'd you talk to today?"

"Lobbyists, mostly."

"Lucky you. I got the cons and ex-cons."

"Sounds like fun. Have you filed your reports yet?" Dave wondered if he'd have time to scan them before going to the Blaine House.

"Why do you ask?" Carl sounded annoyed.

"No reason," Dave said.

"It's late—thought I'd put them in the system tomorrow morning. But I can tell you right now, I didn't get any breaks."

Carl slammed his locker shut and headed for the door. Dave watched him go, wondering if anyone got along with Carl. He stashed his razor in his locker and did a quick mirror check. What was he worried about? Jillian wouldn't care if he arrived with mussed hair. If he could give her the news she wanted to hear, she wouldn't care when he'd last shaved, either. He was a little surprised that he'd taken so much trouble with his appearance. But part of him wasn't surprised at all. Not one bit.

"So, you're not going home this weekend?" Naomi asked.

Jillian looked up from the legal pad where she'd jotted notes about next week's schedule. "No, I thought I'd stay here." Though she missed the house she and Brendon had bought together.

"You've worked hard all week. It wouldn't hurt to have a couple of days at home."

Jillian shrugged. "The EPU thinks I'm safer here."

"They can't make you stay so that it's easier for them."

"No, but I don't like to cause them extra headaches."

Naomi made a face Jillian called her "froufrou face." Usually it meant that Naomi thought she was being too picky.

"Jillian! These people work for you, not the other way around. Their job entails keeping you safe wherever you go. If you want to spend a weekend at home, it's their duty to pack up and go with you."

Jillian pulled out a smile for her old friend. "I have to disagree with you on part of that. I *do* work for them. I work for *all* the people of Maine. If my going home means they have to put in longer hours and spend time away from their families—"

Naomi threw her hands in the air with a snort. "Listen to you! They'll put in just as many hours, whether you're here in Augusta or fifteen miles down the road in Belgrade. And while we're on the subject, I think you've skipped enough social events. You haven't had any problems in the ten days since inauguration day. Will you be going to the reception at Fort Western next weekend, or is that scrubbed, too?"

"I'm not sure yet." Jillian leaned her elbows on her desk and rested her chin on her hands, eyeing her friend uneasily. "I'll let you know after I talk to the EPU agent."

"It doesn't seem fair that you won the election and now you have to give up your social life."

Naomi's attitude surprised Jillian—she wasn't usually so opinionated. When Jillian had entered private legal practice, she'd hired her childhood school chum as a secretary, snatching Naomi away from her job as a waitress. Naomi had soon learned to keep the office running smoothly, just the way Jillian liked it. And Naomi willingly stayed with her when she went into the Maine Senate, managing her home office. Jillian felt an obligation to Naomi. They'd gone through a lot together. Naomi might not be the most government-savvy secretary in Augusta, but she did the job and was loyal, supporting Jillian to the hilt. That was worth a lot.

And now she'd decided to bring Naomi along as personal assistant, to live with her in the Blaine House and handle her social calendar. But Naomi had changed since they'd come to Augusta. In their schooldays, she'd been a mousy girl who never quite edged into the "in crowd." She'd always seemed grateful and surprised that Jillian offered her friendship. Now she seemed more daring, less inhibited. Jillian wasn't sure she liked her friend's transformation. Was it because she'd always taken the lead, and Naomi had followed without question? If so, that certainly didn't paint a pretty picture of her as Naomi's friend.

Naomi smiled. "Sorry. Guess I'm getting antsy. I take about a hundred calls a day from people wanting you to appear at their events."

"You'll have to keep telling them no for the time being, I guess."

Movement at the doorway claimed her attention, and she turned to see Detective Browne on the threshold.

"Detective Hutchins is here, ma'am."

Naomi rose and gathered her notepad and pen. "I'll skedaddle. Do you want coffee sent in?"

"Yes, thanks."

Naomi nodded. "See you at dinner."

As Jillian stood, her stomach fluttered. Tuesday and Friday evenings, when she shared thirty minutes with the rugged detective, had become bright spots in her week. She barely knew Dave Hutchins, and again she wondered if she'd placed too much importance on the time she spent with him. She'd have to be careful not to let her appreciation of the EPU's work transfer to an illogical crush on the investigator.

Dave stood to one side in the hallway and let Naomi exit. To Jillian's surprise, Naomi stopped and looked him over.

"You must be the detective who reports to Jillian on the investigation."

"Uh, yes. I'm David Hutchins."

They shook hands. "Pleased to meet you. I'm the governor's personal assistant, Naomi Plante."

"Miss Plante." Dave bowed his head slightly. Jillian was sure he knew exactly who Naomi was.

Still Naomi lingered. "One of the detectives talked to me last week about the shooting. Your unit is doing a great job, based on what I've seen here at the Blaine House. Of course, I can't speak for Jillian's safety outside this house."

"We're doing everything possible to protect Governor Goff, no matter where she is."

Dave's stock line, Jillian supposed, but she saw them in action day after day. The detectives surrounding her were diligent, to the point that their vigilance sometimes annoyed her. She could never drop her guard without feeling someone was watching or listening. But since their goal was to protect her, she couldn't think of a way to improve the situation.

That didn't mean she was ever one hundred percent safe. As the officers had told her more than once, her life depended in large part on Jillian observing the basic rules the EPU had laid down for her.

Dave came into the office, smiling as his gaze met hers. "Governor."

"Dave, thanks for coming." The next few minutes would be almost private, with only Detective Browne outside the door.

Dave's smile indicated what she might perceive as more than a dutiful greeting or respect for her office. His evident pleasure in seeing her sent a ripple of anticipation through Jillian, and she reminded herself again that this was business.

She held out her hand and he grasped it. "I've ordered a coffee tray."

"Great," he said, their hands clasped just a moment longer than necessary.

She resumed her seat behind the desk, and he pulled a chair in to the opposite side. She wished she'd sat beside him as she had last week, but the truth was, being that close to him had become almost too enjoyable. She needed to focus on the fact that people were trying to kill her, not that Dave had strong, masculine hands or beautiful brown eyes.

"Well, here we are." She smiled in chagrin. "Same old, same old?"

"I'm afraid so. We've managed to eliminate some suspects and tentatively rule out others. But the possibilities are still huge."

"So, what are we focusing on today?"

"Let's revisit one of the routine questions." He fixed her with a sober gaze. "Who is angry with you?"

She raised her shoulders in a helpless shrug.

"Think back. Before the inauguration. Before the election, even. Is there anyone who might feel you stood in their way?"

She dragged her mind back over meetings, cases and causes. "I honestly can't think of anyone."

"All right, let's take a different tack. Who would benefit from your death?"

Memories of the chaos swirling around her after Brendon's accident made her feel a bit queasy. As great as her loss had been, she'd benefited in some ways from her husband's passing. Not just tangible things, like his life insurance. She'd stepped into his Senate seat in Augusta quite easily. She'd gained his political position and the prestige that went with it. Was someone out there hoping to take that away from her?

"Your mother would inherit your estate," he said gently.

"Yes, but . . ." She felt the blood drain from her face. "You couldn't possibly consider my mother a suspect."

"No, I don't. Not seriously. But as a matter of course, the EPU has done a thorough background check on her. I hope you understand."

She pulled in a careful breath. Her legal training told her this was the standard path of an investigation. Spouses and other close relatives were always at the top of the list.

"I do, but you must understand how heartless it feels from where I sit." She put her hand to her forehead and closed her eyes for a moment. "Forgive me. I never realized how draining a legal investigation is for the victim."

"You've had to hold it together constantly while you tend to your other duties—it must be exhausting."

"Exactly." She flashed him a weak smile. "I try not to think about this during the day—it's too distracting. But when I come home at night, it all rushes back to me and I can't think of anything else."

"I'm sorry. I'm sure my visits don't help."

"Actually, they do. When you're here, I put things back in perspective. It reminds me of all that your unit is doing to put an end to the questions and . . . the fear." She caught herself, realizing she hadn't meant to reveal so much to him. But it was so easy to talk to Dave. Too easy.

"You're afraid then?"

"Most of the time, I just keep working. But once in a while it strikes me, and I feel almost paranoid. Someone's out there watching me." She tossed her head and laughed. "That's silly, I guess. I mean, *everyone's* watching me."

He sat forward, leaning on the desk. "Governor . . ." The way he said it, soft and caressing, made her title sound almost like a treasured name. "We're doing everything we can. Everything. And part of that is asking you these difficult questions."

Tears sprang into her eyes, and she looked away from his compelling gaze. "I know. Thank you."

"I hope it will help you to know we've also done a deep background on your personal assistant, and we don't feel she was involved in this."

"I should think not."

"No. But we had to be sure. She's close to you."

Jillian nodded. "Thanks. But Naomi wouldn't benefit from my death. Quite the opposite. And if she wanted to harm me, she'd have much better opportunities than a public press conference." A soft tap at the door drew her attention. "There's our coffee. Come in," she called.

Beth, one of the kitchen staffers, entered with the tray and set it carefully on Jillian's desk.

"Would you like me to pour, ma'am?"

"No, thank you, we're fine."

Beth nodded, smiled and turned to where Andrew Browne still held the door for her. Jillian felt as though she'd just been curtsied to.

The door closed and she looked at Dave. "I'm sorry, but I'm still not used to all this." She waved a hand, encompassing more than just her comfortable office.

His eyes crinkled with humor. "You'll get used to it. Just keep reminding yourself that it's temporary."

"Right. Four years." She lifted the coffeepot and poured for him. She'd had to become an instant hostess when she took up residence in the Blaine House. Though she felt she was off to a good start in steering Maine, she still felt somewhat inadequate in the social realm of her role. "Now, where were we?"

"Who benefits," Dave said.

"Oh. Right." She poured her own mug half-full and took a sip. "Who's on your list, besides Mom?"

"Well, there's the president of the Maine Senate. He would become governor if you died."

Jillian chuckled and offered him the small plate of shortbread cookies. "I'm sorry, but the idea that Parker Tilton would try to kill me is ludicrous. He's antigun. He doesn't hunt. He lives with his sister and two Persian cats. He was standing just to my right during the press conference, and I certainly can't imagine him hiring a hit man to kill me."

Dave grinned. "It was a stretch for me, too."

"Parker and I have been on the opposite sides of the aisle in the Senate for years, but we've always cordially agreed to disagree on political issues."

"I'll take that as an endorsement for Senator Tilton."

She set her mug on the desk. "Dave, why would someone want to kill me? It makes no sense to me."

He sat still for a moment, looking at her. "Perhaps someone from your past is using your new political status as cover to kill you."

Jillian frowned. "Why?"

"To make it look like a political assassination, when it's actually related to something else."

Jillian sighed. "This all just makes me want to go out in public even more, to show that I haven't been beaten by this."

"Don't ever go out of this house alone. Always be sure your security team is in place before you interview someone in private, even in this room. And be careful about letting yourself be seen at the windows—"

"Dave, I know. I know. I'm just . . . day-dreaming."

He smiled apologetically. "I regret being the one to make you think about unpleasant things."

She gazed into his brown eyes, startled by his honesty. "You don't, Dave. Quite the contrary actually. I feel very safe with you." It was out of her mouth before she could stop it, and she regretted it instantly. But Dave met her gaze and held it.

"I'm honored," he said. She felt heat flush her cheeks, and she forced herself to look away before she said anything else.

FIVE

Jillian looked over her list of Tuesday appointments. A full day as usual, and she would leave for Portland at 5:00 p.m. to attend a dinner hosted by the Cumberland County Republican Committee. She closed her eyes for a moment and rubbed her eyelids. She'd probably fall asleep in the car tonight.

"Does everything look all right, ma'am?" Lettie Wheeler asked. She had worked in the governor's office for eight years, and Jillian had accepted her predecessor's recommendation and kept her on. Lettie knew the ins and outs of protocol, official etiquette and legislative procedure. While Naomi presided over the governor's social calendar, Lettie handled everything related to state business. After only three weeks in office, Jillian knew she couldn't survive without her.

"It's fine. A bit tight this afternoon, but we'll cope."

"If you don't mind my saying so, you look a bit tired today, ma'am."

Jillian tried not to frown. "Lettie, you sound like my mother."

"Is your mother right?"

"I suppose so. My adrenaline kept me going for a while, but the strain is catching up to me."

The older woman nodded sagely. "It's a demanding life. And the speaking and travel schedule will get heavier as we head into spring. You need to guard your time to rest."

Jillian gave her a sheepish smile. "Thanks."

"A lot of people are praying for you, Governor," Lettie murmured.

"Thank you. I'll remember that tonight if I can't sleep again."

Lettie put her pen behind her ear so that the business end stuck out from among her silvery curls. "Right. Now then, today's program. At ten forty-five, your driver will arrive to take you to the paper mill in Shawmut. Then you'll return home for lunch and come back here to meet with the majority leader about the water quality proposal. I'll try to hustle your other afternoon appointments along a bit so we can get you off in time for your trip to Portland."

"Thank you." Jillian always had trouble cutting off visits with people who came to consult her or sought her attention for their causes. "I'll do my best not to lag behind schedule, too."

When Lettie smiled, her eyes twinkled. "I've spoken to Miss Plante, and she'll make sure your gown, shoes and jewelry are ready for this evening."

Jillian cringed. She didn't like it when her staff

hovered—even if it was just Naomi. "I can dress myself."

Lettie closed her notebook and rose. "Of course you can. But with a schedule as packed as yours, it will help to have things ready when you get over to the Blaine House. If you don't want Miss Plante or one of the maids to help you dress, just shoo them out."

So she did understand. Jillian reached to squeeze her hand. "Thank you, Lettie. I know Naomi and all of the staff try to make my job easier, but my independent habits are hard to kick. Since Brendon died, I've done everything for myself." She didn't mention that since the election things had changed between her and Naomi. There were things she couldn't discuss with her friend now, and the easy banter between them had lessened.

Lettie pursed her lips, but her faded blue eyes still twinkled. "I'd never have said this to the last governor—he wouldn't have taken it well at all—but my dear, just give yourself permission to let others pamper you a little. You'll be surprised at how much smoother things will be."

Jillian chuckled. "You may be right. Thank you."

Lettie nodded, businesslike again.

"Oh, and Lettie . . ." Jillian glanced at the printed schedule again. "Detective Hutchins is supposed to report to me at 6:00 p.m. on

Tuesdays. We need to tell him I won't be in tonight."

"Shall I call him?"

"Yes. Or maybe . . ." She hesitated, then looked up at Lettie. "I suppose I could see him when we get back. I'd hate to wait until Friday."

"I'll call him. Now, I expect your nine o'clock appointment is cooling his heels in the outer office. Ready?"

"Ready." As her assistant left the room, Jillian inhaled deeply. A lobbyist for the semiconductor business—Maine's most lucrative export at the moment—wanted fifteen minutes of her time. That fifteen minutes would be much more enjoyable if she could spend it with the diligent and sympathetic detective. She sat up straight as the door opened again. She'd better get her mind off the handsome officer and onto computers.

Dave arrived at the Blaine House at nine that evening, though the governor's driver had phoned to say that their expected time of arrival was nine-thirty. He entered through the back entrance and found Detective Bob Caruthers on duty in the security office.

"How's it going?" Bob asked.

"Oh, middlin'." Dave didn't like admitting that the leads were petering out. He and Carl Millbridge were still spending forty or more hours a week investigating the inauguration day shooting, but the other officers of the EPU had been assigned to other duties. There had been no new attacks, but their lack of a resolution on the shooting frustrated him terribly.

"The governor's meeting with you tonight?" Bob asked.

"Yes. It's later than usual, but I don't mind." Dave unzipped his jacket, hoping his ears weren't turning scarlet. His admiration for Jillian had soared since he'd begun meeting with her, but Bob didn't need to know that. Maybe he could blame his flush on the frigid temperature outside.

"Well, they'll come in right there." Bob nodded down the hall toward the back entrance.

"There's no one with the governor tonight, is there?"

"In her car? Just Browne. He's driving her tonight."

Dave nodded. He looked at his watch. Quarter past nine. "Guess I'll go outside. They could be a little early."

"It's cold out there. He'll call when he gets off I-95."

Dave was just antsy to see her and to know she'd arrived safely. Portland was as far as she'd traveled since taking the oath of office, and it was only fifty miles away. Next week, if the clear weather held, she was scheduled to speak at the University of Maine in Presque Isle, more than two hundred miles to the north. A squad of four EPU agents would accompany her. Not that the potato farmers in Aroostook County would be likely to make trouble, but you never knew. Get the governor out of town, away from her usual surroundings, and anything could happen. The shooter they'd failed to catch might see it as a good opportunity to strike again.

"Want coffee?" Bob asked.

Dave shook his head and paced to the window. No doubt Jillian would order coffee sent up to her private office for the two of them. He looked toward the corner where Andrew would turn. Traffic was light on Capitol Street. Up a few blocks were several shopping centers, but it was late enough that most shoppers had already headed home.

At nine twenty-five, Andrew called to announce their approach. Dave walked down the hallway and out into the cold night air. Stars spattered the sky overhead.

An SUV slowed and turned in at the driveway on Grove Street. Dave stood where he thought Jillian's door would be when Andrew stopped the vehicle. A few seconds later, her warm voice greeted him.

"Dave! Thank you. I shouldn't have kept you out so late."

"It's a pleasure, ma'am."

She placed her gloved hand in his. By the time

63

Andrew got around the vehicle, she was standing beside Dave on the driveway.

"Thank you, Andrew," Jillian said. "Good night." She smiled up at Dave and stepped away from the SUV's open door, the starlight reflecting off her glossy hair. "Shall we go in?"

"Yes," Dave said, forcing himself to stop admiring her.

Andrew began to swing the door shut behind her. A *ping* rang out in the crisp night, followed by a distant *pow*. Dave's adrenaline surged. He reached past her and grabbed the edge of the door, throwing it open again, against Andrew's push. He shoved Jillian backward, onto the seat of the SUV.

"Get in! Keep your head down!"

She obeyed without question, scrambling onto the backseat. Dave slammed the door and threw himself on the ground next to the vehicle. Andrew crouched beside him, his gun drawn. All was still. For a millisecond it was too much like Iraq.

"Was that what I think it was?" Andrew asked.

Dave focused on the present and Jillian's safety. "Gunshot. I think it hit the vehicle."

"From the statehouse?"

"No." Dave edged up until he could peek through the SUV's windows. Jillian huddled inside, barely visible in the shadows. Beyond, a block to the west, lights shone on top of the parking garage.

"Up there." He nodded up the street. "On the garage roof."

"Are you sure?"

Dave hesitated. "Ninety percent."

Andrew pulled out his radio. "I'll get backup and send officers up there."

"They'll be too late." Dave's breath formed a white cloud in the frosty air. "We've got to get the governor into the house."

"Hey, what's going on?" Bob Caruthers called from the house door.

"We've got a shooter on the parking garage," Dave yelled. "Andrew called for backup. We'll bring the governor inside through the dining room entrance."

"Got it."

"Get in from this side and drive around to the family dining room entrance," Dave said to Andrew. "Get as close as you can to the steps. I'll get her into the house."

"Can do." Andrew reached for the door handle.

"Hey," Dave said softly, "keep down, will ya?"

"Sure." The night was still, except for distant traffic and a faraway horn. Andrew yanked the front door open. "Governor, I'm getting in," he said, still crouching. "I'll drive around back and Detective Hutchins will assist you into the house."

"All right." Jillian's voice came soft but steady.

Dave eased away from the vehicle, bent over, and bounded around the corner of the mansion's back wing to the marble steps outside the rear entrance to the dining room. He watched the vehicle come around with the lights off, and stop inches from the steps. A glance to his left told Dave they were shielded from view, even if the shooter was on top of the four-story parking garage up the hill.

He dashed forward and opened Jillian's door. Once more, she stepped out, this time ducking low. Dave shielded her with his body and they made their way quickly up the steps. Bob held the door open with the room darkened. As soon as they were inside, Bob secured the door and put the lights on. They dashed through the dining room to the hallway.

"This way." Dave took her to the front stairs. Jillian paused at the bottom of the flight, panting.

"Are you all right?" Dave asked.

Her lips trembled and her warm breath fanned his chin. "Yes, I'm fine."

"Let's get you upstairs then, and in a secure place."

Naomi soon joined them in the family living room, anxious to see that Jillian was all right. She summoned a maid to run a hot bath for the governor and took Jillian to the master suite.

As soon as Detective Penny Thurlow arrived to stay with them in the private quarters, Dave went back downstairs. Bob was directing a rapid investigation from the security office in the rear wing. Andrew clapped Dave on the shoulder as he entered.

"You and me, up to the garage? There are half a dozen patrol officers there already."

"Let's go."

Bob covered his telephone receiver with one hand. "You're in charge, Hutchins. They haven't let anyone drive out of the garage."

"Right. We'll handle it."

"Leave the SUV here," Bob called after them. "We need to check it for damage and get the projectile angle."

Dave and Andrew jumped into Dave's pickup. Dave turned on the strobe light. In less than a minute, they entered the garage and were flagged down by the first responding Augusta police officer.

"We've got two men at each exit and four more available to help you search. More on the way."

Dave immediately deployed the men. Only two dozen cars were parked on the first level, and a few more on the second. Stairways and elevators required systematic searches. While Andrew saw to the details, Dave ran up the stairs to the open third level of the structure. The fourth level covered only a small part of the third, and he could see no one up there.

Dave hurried to the east side and looked down past a low retaining wall, over a bank and its parking lot, beyond the shrubs and leafless trees, to the driveway and yard of the Blaine House.

The colonial-style mansion sparkled as white as the snow around it in the glow of security lights. Several cars sat near the staff entrance. Dave walked slowly along the wall until he came to the spot that gave the best view of the private back driveway, the Blaine House stable, which now functioned as a garage, and the private entrance to the house.

During his first week as an EPU officer, he had climbed up here and contemplated the parking garage's advantages as a sniper's post. Nearly a hundred and thirty years ago, James G. Blaine was almost killed by a shooter in the Capitol dome, across the street from the mansion. Nowadays, security at the Capitol was so tight that it would be nearly impossible for an assassin to repeat that escapade. But the parking garage was open to anyone. They'd talked about it once in an EPU briefing. Short of convincing the legislature to budget funds to raise the height of the wall, he didn't see what could be done about it. The garage provided a perfect view, especially in winter, with tree branches stripped of their foliage. It was a long shot, but with a good scope and a bipod, very doable.

Dave pictured himself standing beside the SUV, opening Jillian's door. In the light from the vehicle, he'd seen only her loveliness, though once they were inside the fatigue and stress had shown in the lines of her face. He'd just begun to know her. Was he just dazzled by a beautiful celebrity who depended on him? No, he was past that. His admiration grew with each new thing he learned about her. After only a few weeks, he cared about her more than he'd ever cared for any other person under his protection.

He took his flashlight from his belt and stooped, shining the powerful beam along the floor.

Anything, Lord. I'll take anything right now. A gum wrapper, a cigarette butt. Just give me some direction. Please!

Burnished metal glowed in the beam of his light. Dave reached into his inside jacket pocket for latex gloves and an evidence bag.

The door to the stairway creaked open. Dave looked toward the figure silhouetted against the rectangle of light.

"Over here, Andrew."

His colleague strode toward him. "We've combed every inch of this building. Nothing. If he was up here, he got out fast and clean."

"Well, maybe this will make you feel better." Dave straightened and carefully held up his find, an empty brass shell casing.

SIX

"Mom, I'm okay. Really." Jillian sank down onto her four-poster bed and held the phone an inch from her ear as her mother alternately wailed and scolded. She wished she'd put off calling until after breakfast.

"But they shot at you again! The police have got to do something! I knew I should have stayed with you longer."

"They're doing something. They're out looking for the gunman right now. For all I know, they may have caught him."

"But what if they haven't? You should ask the FBI to come in."

Jillian gritted her teeth and stood. "I have to get to my office. Look, why don't you come down for supper? We can talk about this then."

"What are they serving tonight?"

"Mom, I don't know, okay? Just come." A tap on her door gave her an excuse to end the conversation with a quick, "Gotta go. See ya."

"Hi. Sorry to bother you so early." Naomi stood in the doorway wearing black slacks and a teal sweater set. "Lettie Wheeler called to say that Colonel Smith is coming here to brief you in person at nine o'clock. She's coming over to help you with some correspondence until the colonel arrives."

Jillian opened her mouth and closed it again. She walked to the door of her dressing room. "I guess this means today's not the day they let me start walking to the statehouse, huh?"

"Not on your life."

She sighed. "Okay. Can you come fix my necklace for me? I never can hook this one by myself."

Naomi followed her into the dressing room. "You know, you could redecorate this room so that it would look more feminine. Half the first ladies who preceded you redecorated the family quarters."

Jillian shrugged and held out the pendant. "I don't mind it."

Naomi huffed out a little breath. "Masculine. Gray striped wallpaper. How about a few ruffles and flowers?"

Jillian chuckled and turned her back. "Let me get used to living here first."

Naomi fastened the chain for her. "All set."

Jillian snagged a portfolio on her way past the Victorian secretary in her bedroom. "What are we having for dinner tonight? I *am* eating here, right?"

"Yes, and you asked for onion pie."

"Oops. Mom hates that."

"Your mother's coming?"

"Yeah, I invited her to keep her from screaming at me about last night's shooting."

"Want me to switch it with tomorrow night's menu?"

Jillian grimaced as they headed down the stairs. "I hate to put Amelia out."

"Get a grip, girl. Asking your chef to change one dish is not a major executive decision. Now, go get your oatmeal. If Amelia can't do it, I'll ask her to cook a chicken breast for your mom."

"Thanks."

After breakfast, Jillian carried her cup of tea to her office. She hated to keep people waiting, and efficient Lettie would already be there.

"Good morning, Lettie." She smiled at the older woman. Lettie's cheery red silk blouse matched her lipstick.

"Good morning, Governor."

"I'm sorry your routine was disrupted this morning."

Lettie's sunny smile made the room seem a little brighter. "Oh, don't worry about me. I can crack the whip just as smartly here or at the Capitol." She glanced about the well-appointed office. "I haven't been in this room for almost a year. You've kept it just the way the last governor had it."

Jillian swallowed a laugh. "So far. But if Naomi has her way, I'll do some redecorating before I leave the Blaine House." She sat down behind the desk and set her mug on a coaster.

Lettie held up a stack of papers. "If you're ready to begin work, I have some items that need your signature. Then we'll go through some requests that have come in for appointments. I've put off scheduling you too heavily, but if you think you can handle a full day in Oxford County next week . . ."

"We should wait and see what Colonel Smith has to say. I have a feeling he's going to chain me to this house until they catch the person who's trying to shoot me."

"Oh, dear." Lettie's face crumpled for a moment, but she regained her placid expression in a matter of seconds. "I'm so sorry you're going through this. It's a real burden, especially right at the start of your term, when you want to show your supporters that they chose wisely."

An officer knocked and announced that Colonel Smith had arrived before Jillian could respond.

Lettie tucked the papers into a folder. "I'll wait downstairs."

The colonel entered. Dapper, as usual, in a three-piece suit. He inclined his head toward Lettie as she exited.

"How are you, Colonel?" Jillian asked.

"I'm fine, thanks, ma'am. The question is, how are *you* this morning?"

Jillian hoped her predawn hours of tossing weren't detectable. "I'm well, thank you. I trust you've brought me some news about the little incident last night?" She gestured toward a chair and resumed her place at her desk.

Smith cleared his throat. "Yes, I do have some information. Our officers have reconstructed the shooting."

She studied him while she reviewed in her mind the moment when they'd heard the gunshot and Dave had pushed her unceremoniously into the SUV. "So, what did their efforts tell you?"

Smith opened the leather folder he had brought with him and looked down at a legal pad inside. "The shooter was indeed on the roof of the parking garage up the street, as my men suspected. They retrieved a shell casing last night, and we're running tests on it right now." He glanced up at her. "He was trying to shoot at you over the top of the vehicle. Because you exited on the side nearer the house, he had to wait until you took a step away from the SUV. His bullet hit the roof and deflected. He missed you by inches."

Jillian's mouth went dry. "That close?"

"I strongly suggest you curtail your public appearances. Do your office work here in the Blaine House for a few days until we run this fellow down."

She nodded, still at a loss for words. "Excuse me just a minute." She rose and went into the next room. In one corner, an armoire concealed a television set and a small refrigerator. She opened the minifridge and selected a bottle of Poland Spring water. When she turned, Colonel Smith stood in the connecting doorway.

"I'm sorry," he said sheepishly. "But you really need to have an officer with you at all times." He glanced toward the windows. "And these curtains are wide open. Last night's attack underscored what we already knew. No matter how closely we guard you, there will be moments of opportunity for someone who seeks them."

She walked past him, trying not to glare. She sat down and twisted the cap off the bottle. The cool water bathed her parched throat, and she set the bottle down. The colonel resumed his seat facing her.

"You know, Colonel, I appreciate you and the state police. The officers of the EPU have been wonderful, and I feel safe with them. But I'm starting to feel a little claustrophobic."

"That's understandable."

"Before the election, I imagined myself living here and walking across the street every morning to my office in the Capitol."

He shook his head before half the sentence was out of her mouth. "We can't let you do that."

"I know. But I also know that I can't hide in this building. I need to show the people of Maine that our government is strong, and that I won't let my duties go unfulfilled until everything is perfect. That could take some time."

His face flushed, and he fiddled with the folder. "I'm sure this will break soon. With the new evidence—"

"And the new attack," she reminded him. "The new evidence doesn't bear on the inauguration day shooting, does it?"

"Well, not directly."

"We have no proof that the two shooters were the same person, do we?"

He shifted in his chair. "Technically, no, but—"

"I need fresh air, Colonel. I cower in a heavily guarded bunker."

"But Governor, just getting you from here to the statehouse without exposing you to danger is a challenge."

"One I'm sure the fine men and women of the EPU can meet."

He raised his chin to speak again when his phone trilled. He winced and stood to fumble in the pocket of his trousers. "I'm sorry. That's my emergency phone. They wouldn't call me on this line if it weren't important."

"Take it, by all means." She swiveled her chair slightly away from him and reached for her water bottle.

"Smith here," he said gruffly. "Oh, Hutchins. What have you got?"

Dave. Jillian's morning instantly grew sunnier. She stood and went to the window, looking down over the snowy yard and the white fence that separated the front gardens from the street. If Smith weren't on the phone, he'd probably scold her and tell her not to endanger herself like that. In fact, she was surprised he hadn't suggested moving her Blaine House office across the hall into one of the guest rooms in the back.

"I see," Smith said. "Yes. Where are you now?"

Across the street, the state office building loomed huge and gray, and beyond it the Capitol dome rose, glorious in the dazzling winter sun. Dave was out there working on her case, diligent as always. Jillian wondered if he'd slept at all.

"I'm with the governor," the colonel said. "Why don't you come up here and give her these findings yourself?"

Jillian wiped the grin off her face before she turned to face him. "Good news, I hope?"

"Maybe. I told Hutchins to come up and report in person. He and Detective Millbridge have finished their calculations."

Two minutes later, Bob Caruthers tapped on the door and admitted Dave.

"Good morning, Governor."

Jillian noticed the lines at the corners of his eyes looked deeper, and he hadn't shaved. In fact—yes, that was the same shirt and tie he'd worn last night. The man hadn't even slept.

"I hope you got some rest, Detective," she said, concerned.

"Carl Millbridge and I wanted to get as much data as we could while the evidence was fresh."

She sat down and indicated that he take the chair opposite his colonel. "What did you find?"

"Last night we discovered an empty cartridge casing on top of the parking garage. The mark on the roof of the SUV was probably made by a bullet fired from up there. We were able to put the vehicle back in the exact spot it was in when the shot was fired, and we've measured the angle of the projectile based on the ding it left on the SUV."

The colonel leaned forward. "And?"

"I wish I could tell you something definite. Like height. Because of the distance, and variables like wind, gun model and cartridge load, we can't say for sure. But the shooter didn't kneel and rest his rifle on the wall. If our calculations are accurate, in order to fire a rifle from up there and hit your vehicle from that angle and that range, the shooter had to be at least five feet, ten inches tall."

Jillian sank back in her chair and exhaled. "So. That narrows it down some."

Dave chuckled. "It could eliminate ninety percent of women and Parker Tilton." He glanced at the colonel, who scowled at him.

Jillian hid her smirk behind her hand. The Senate president stood only five feet six inches with his shoes on.

Dave continued quickly. "Anyway, we can't be positive, but I'm banking on it being a tall man."

Jillian nodded. "So, what now?"

"The casing is undergoing laboratory tests, and the SUV has gone to the lab, too, to see if they can find out anything else. We've got a man with a metal detector searching the area near the driveway for the bullet."

"Nothing yet?" Smith asked.

"No. We're going to talk to people who parked in the garage last night and see if anyone saw a man on the roof or in the stairway."

"He took a risk carrying a rifle up there," Smith mused.

"True. He may have driven up to the top level, but it would have taken a couple of minutes to get down, in that case. I think he parked nearby and walked up, then ran down the stairwell after he fired. He got away before the first officer responded, about four minutes after Browne's call."

"Four minutes." Colonel Smith's eyebrows drew together in a fuzzy wedge.

Dave nodded regretfully. "Browne or I could probably have gotten there sooner, but our first priority was to get the governor safely into the house. By the time she was secure, two Augusta police officers were on the scene."

"I don't suppose there were any fingerprints," Jillian said.

Dave shook his head. "A partial from the casing, but we haven't been able to make a match yet."

They all sat in silence for several seconds. A glance at Dave's somber face revealed his frustration and disappointment.

Jillian sat forward and addressed the colonel. "Well, sir, it sounds as though the EPU is in high gear. Thank you for coming in person to report to me. I assume the Public Safety Department's spokesman has briefed the press."

Smith almost growled. "Did you see the morning news?"

"No, I didn't. Should I have?"

Smith shrugged. "Mark Payson gave them the basics, but of course all the reporters want more. I'll have Detective Millbridge talk to them this afternoon, so they'll have something fresh on the evening news." He stood, and Dave jumped out of his chair. "I'd best be going. Are you finished, Hutchins?"

Dave hesitated. "The unit needs to know if the governor has changed her schedule for the next twenty-four hours."

"Absolutely." Smith stared pointedly at Jillian. "I'd like you to stay in this building today, ma'am. It will make it easier for us to do our work."

She sighed and rose from her chair. "I suppose I'd better call Mrs. Wheeler back in here to go over the schedule. Perhaps you could stay a moment, Detective?"

"Of course," Dave said.

Colonel Smith tucked his folder under his arm, nodded at Jillian, and left the room. She let out a pent-up breath. Dave took a step toward her, then stopped. They stood looking at each other for a long moment.

"I'm so sorry this happened," he said at last.

"Thank you." She managed a smile. "You need to sleep, Dave."

"I'll take the rest of today off. But I'd like to come by again this evening and check on you, if you don't mind."

"I don't. I'd appreciate it if you'd update me on what the unit accomplishes today. Oh, and my mother will be here." She grimaced. "Mom doesn't take these things lightly. I'm sure it will help if she can get an official word from you."

"I'd be happy to talk to her."

Jillian nodded. She wished they were standing closer, without the big walnut desk between them.

A light tap on the door preceded Lettie's entrance. "Hello again. Ah, Detective Hutchins. I'm told you'll take a copy of Governor Goff's schedule back to the EPU office."

"Yes, ma'am," Dave said. "That will help us plan surveillance for today and tonight."

As Lettie laid her papers on the desk and pulled up a chair, Dave looked at Jillian. The look in his eyes made her heart lurch against her will. There was no turning back now, and she knew it. She was falling for her protector, which was absolutely the last thing she should be doing. But she could no more change her feelings for him than turn back time.

SEVEN

A week after the second shooting incident, Dave's ringing phone woke him.

"Can you help me out, Dave? The governor's determined to slip the leash this morning."

"Penny?"

"Yeah, I'm at the Blaine House."

"What's up?"

"She's got cabin fever, that's what. In a twenty-seven-room mansion."

Dave sat up and rubbed the back of his neck. "What's she doing?"

"She insists she's going over to the statehouse. I've tried to convince her to wait until Monday, but she's determined to get back to what she calls 'normal' today."

"Let her."

A silence of several seconds followed. "You sure?"

"Yeah, but keep at least two officers with her, with two more standing by while you transfer her over there. In and out of the car quickly."

"Okay. If you think so."

Dave sighed. "The governor's right. She can't stay sequestered and be an effective leader."

"I was hoping you'd talk her into waiting."

Dave pushed the covers aside and swung his legs over the side of the bed. "What makes you think she'd listen to me? Right now she needs to feel she has some measure of control. She doesn't want to give this guy the satisfaction of making her a weak governor."

"Dave, she's scared."

"She'd be crazy if she weren't. But she's still going forward. That's courage, and that's the attitude that will send her down in history as one of our most capable governors."

"Wow, you're a real fan, aren't you?" Penny asked.

"Aren't you?"

"Haven't made up my mind yet. But okay, I'll tell her she can have her way. I suppose you'll drop by tonight to give her an update?"

"Yeah. Such as it is." What he wouldn't give right now for something significant to tell her.

Dave was laboring without success to find more evidence. Though Carl Millbridge technically headed the investigation, Dave spent more time in the field and felt he was closer to the case. Carl did more of the telephone interviews and oversaw the laboratory tests, while Dave scoured the capital area, digging for clues.

Each morning Dave awoke to face failure. Until the shooter was in custody, nothing could be counted as success. Three weeks after the second shooting incident, they were no closer to making an arrest.

He approached his Tuesday evening meeting with the printout of his assignments for the week folded in his inside pocket. He was to have Friday off and arrive for duty late Saturday at the Blaine House.

"Dave, it's good to see you again," Jillian said as he entered her cozy office at the mansion.

"Thank you. You're looking well." He clasped her hand for a moment and released it reluctantly, then sat down opposite her. "There's something I wanted to talk to you about."

"What's that?"

"You're planning to go to Orono Saturday evening."

She picked up the silver pen from her desk and flipped it back and forth rapidly. "Yes. I think it's time I ventured farther afield. We've cancelled enough appearances."

"But a concert an hour and a half away?"

"The Bangor Symphony is playing at the Maine Center for the Arts. I planned this outing months ago."

He shook his head. "I urge you not to risk appearing in public again so soon."

"You know my feelings about that." Her blue eyes flashed. "Nothing happened to me in Portland. It was my arrival back here that gave the shooter his opportunity. That happens every day. He could try again anytime."

"Nighttime is easier. It's harder to see clearly. Fewer witnesses. There weren't many people at the garage that night to see him go up there and wait for you to come home."

"That's true. I assume you'll post a man or two at the garage Saturday night to make sure no one tries it again."

"You bet your boots we will. If I can't persuade you to stay home, that is."

"You can't." She locked eyes with him, and for the first time he felt the steel he'd guessed she possessed. One more thing to admire about her, even if it would make his job harder. "I need to be there. I've encouraged financial grants to the arts, and it's imperative that I show my support." Her voice cracked just a little, and she cleared her throat.

Dave linked his hands together and leaned forward. "All right. I'll be driving. We'll put you in the Lincoln this time with Penny Thurlow."

"Senator Armstrong is going with me. He's a dear old friend."

"Yes, I saw his name on the list. Penny will ride up front with me. You and the senator will sit in the backseat."

She nodded, saying nothing.

"We'll put two more officers in the SUV. They'll go ahead of us as we leave Augusta. We may switch back and forth on I-95, depending on how the situation feels, but I'll be in constant touch with Andrew."

"Andrew being the other driver?"

"Correct. Ryan Mills will be with him. And when we get to Orono, they'll drive into the parking lot first. I'll take you right up to the door. Andrew and Ryan will be ready to shield you between the car and the door of the building. You will go in quickly, without stopping to chat or wave. Clear?"

"Yes, sir." She smiled faintly.

He answered her smile, wishing she could enjoy the event the way she wanted to instead of worrying about her safety. "Ryan will take up his position at the entrance to your box. Andrew and Penny will stick to you like glue. Orono police will also be on hand. I will park the car and stay outside for the first half of the program. Then Andrew will come out and spell me, and I'll join you inside."

She frowned and tapped her pen on the desk. "One of you has to stay outside during the entire concert?"

"Yes. We've got to make sure no one is messing with the vehicles."

Her eyes narrowed. "It will be cold."

"Don't worry about us. Visitors will be allowed to greet you in the box during the intermission, provided they're on our preapproved list."

Her jaw dropped. "You have a list of people you'll let talk to me?"

"At a public event, on a public university campus, after two attempts on your life? Yes."

She sighed.

"It's not as bad as it sounds. Our office is doing background checks on at least forty people who want to see you—everyone from students to university bigwigs. Toward the end of the intermission, you'll be allowed to stand at the front of the box for thirty seconds and wave to the crowd."

"Like the queen?"

"Exactly. I don't like it, but Colonel Smith says you've got to have a chance to connect with the people. Approximately fifteen minutes before the program is over, we'll get you and Armstrong out to the SUV, and I'll drive you home. Andrew will follow in the Lincoln."

"We don't get to stay until the end of the concert?" Jillian's voice ratcheted up with protest. "There's a reception following."

"Madam Governor, this is for your safety. We've notified the organizers that you won't be able to attend the party. If all goes well, perhaps you can appear at a reception following the next public event you attend. But not this time."

"It's a test."

"Of sorts." He maintained his unswerving gaze, which was easy to do because he was looking at an incredibly beautiful woman. He could only hope the look on his face was all business.

At last she nodded, her mouth compressed. "All right. I know you're trying to do what's best for me. I guess I should be glad I'm not running into solid opposition on this."

"Governor, if we had caught—"

She waved a hand and looked away. "No, you're absolutely right. We need to do it this way. And Dave, thanks for all you've done already. I *do* appreciate it."

He nodded, relieved. She was, after all, in charge. She could insist on going out in public. She could even dismiss the EPU. He didn't think she would be that foolish, though he knew she chafed at their constant presence.

She inhaled through her nose, pulling her shoulders back as she did. "So. Anything new you can tell me about the shootings?"

"We know the type of rifle he used, but not the make. We have no witnesses. This guy is good. We don't even know if he drove into the garage or not."

"No video from the garage that night."

"The camera at the main entrance was down, and it had been for a few days."

"Why wasn't it fixed?"

Dave sighed in frustration. "That's what we'd like to know. I'm sure Detective Millbridge has made someone somewhere extremely uncomfortable over that. But if the shooter put it out of commission, why didn't he wait to do it until the day he shot at you? The chances of its being repaired were high."

Jillian's eyes widened. "Maybe he planned to strike earlier. Maybe he was up there a couple of nights before, but I didn't present him with a target. Surely he went up to look the place over and see if it was a good spot for his purposes."

"Yes. I've thought about that. The night he shot at you was the first night in more than a week that you'd gone out and come in fairly late. He might have waited on other evenings for an opportunity."

"Or he might have gained access to my schedule."

Dave hated to admit it, but she was right. "Yes, that's possible."

Her whole body shook as she exhaled. Dave wished more than ever that protocol did not stand between them. Against his better judgment, he reached across the desk and put his hand on hers. She met his gaze with a warmth in her eyes that made him want to pull her into his arms.

"You're doing great," he said softly. "We're going to get to the bottom of this."

Former Senator Joseph Armstrong cut an imposing figure in his tuxedo. Dave took the silver-haired icon's measure as they waited in the reception room for Jillian. Three terms in Washington and many years of service to Maine before that, as commissioner of economic development and then attorney general. He was highly respected in local, state and federal circles and served on the board of at least five corporations, though he'd officially listed himself as "retired" for ten years. He'd turned down a nomination by the last governor for State of Maine Supreme Court Justice.

"I understand you've known the governor for a long time, sir." Dave stood with the senator before one of the fireplaces with a glass of iced tea in his hand. Jillian had apparently instructed the staff that she wanted no alcohol served in the mansion during her tenure. Dave didn't mind, but that news didn't sit as well with Armstrong. Dave flicked a glance every few seconds toward the door that led into the sunroom. Detective Ryan Mills stood near the doorway on the east end of the room, unobtrusively watching the hall beyond.

"Yes, I took Brendon Goff under my wing when he was still in law school. He clerked for me for a short time, and he was one of the best clerks I've ever had. And Jillian—well, she was just as bright. A shining star."

Dave smiled. "They made a stellar couple, I guess."

The senator nodded gravely. "Unbounded potential in those two. Brendon's death was a terrible blow, not only for those who knew him. This country lost a potential statesman of unknown scope."

"Yes," Dave murmured.

Armstrong sipped his drink and focused on the far doorway. "Ah, but we still have Jillian."

Dave smiled. "Indeed we do, sir."

"I'm sure she has a brilliant future ahead. I've advised her occasionally these last couple of years. She's come to me with a few questions as to how to get things done without ruffling too many feathers. Not that she'd be opposed to ruffling feathers." Armstrong chuckled. "I've told her more than once to be patient and not expect to change policy overnight."

Dave considered that. He understood from the news reports he'd read and even their private conversations that Jillian hoped to leave her mark during her administration. She was bent on bringing the state's economy to a healthier level. Maine had suffered economic depression long enough.

"I just hope you boys can keep her safe so she can to do some good."

"Yes, sir. We're being extravigilant."

"Jillian should be able to go out and enjoy an evening, but still—can't say I'm a hundred percent confident she ought to just now, with this lunatic on the loose."

Andrew stepped into the hall, and Dave heard a low murmur of voices. A moment later, Penny Thurlow entered, dressed in a form-fitting black dress and stiletto heels. Her short-cropped hair looked glossier than usual, and a chunky crystal necklace glittered at her throat.

"Hello, Penny," Dave said. "Have you met Senator Armstrong?"

"Oh, it's former Senator," the older man said with a gentle smile. "I'm just 'Mister' now. Surely you're not one of our bodyguards tonight?"

"Yes, she is," Dave replied. "This is Detective Penny Thurlow of the EPU. She'll ride with us and stay near the governor throughout the evening."

Armstrong took her hand and bowed slightly. "Pleased to meet you. I can't say I've ever had such a lovely escort."

"Thank you." Penny flushed a bit. "I hope you'll have an enjoyable evening."

"How could it be otherwise with *two* lovely ladies along? I can't imagine a boring evening with Jillian and—Ah, here she is." The older man's face lit.

Dave turned and caught his breath. Jillian greeted Andrew with a friendly smile that clearly bedazzled the detective. Her cobalt-blue gown fit her to perfection and brought out the striking blue of her eyes. Her golden hair was caught up in a simple but elegant knot, showcasing her long neck and delicately chiseled cheekbones.

Jillian looked toward them and smiled at Dave—no, past him, at Senator Armstrong. He tried to ignore the flat disappoint that hit him as she strode toward the old man. She bypassed the hand Armstrong held out and embraced him.

"Well, my dear, don't you look fine."

"It's wonderful to see you again, Joe." Jillian disentangled herself from the senator's arms and extended her hand to Penny. "Penny. I'm glad you're coming with us. You look lovely."

"Thank you," Penny murmured, her eyes downcast as she shook hands with the governor.

"Dave." Jillian paused. He felt a rush as she appraised him and he found himself hoping that he met her standards of dress for the evening. "I'm glad you'll be with us."

He took her hand, conscious of the eyes upon them, careful not to squeeze her fingers too intimately or hold on too long.

"Thank you, ma'am. I must say, you look stunning."

Jillian chuckled. "Thanks. I confess, I felt less tired when I put this dress on." She looked back toward Armstrong with a sly smile. "I haven't had a date for years."

He flushed pink and stepped forward, his face wreathed in smiles. "Well, my dear, would you like a drink first, or shall we begin our journey?"

Jillian glanced at her watch. "I think we'd better head for Orono, hadn't we?" When her gaze met his, Dave again felt a distinct connection that went far deeper than the question she'd asked.

"Anytime you're ready, Governor."

Armstrong crooked his elbow for Jillian to grasp. "Well, then, shall we? I'm sure these gentlemen—and lady—" He nodded deferentially at Penny "—will direct us in how they'd like this to go."

Dave smiled. "Yes, sir. We're going out the front entrance, onto State Street."

He looked around for Andrew, caught his eye and nodded. Andrew adjusted the transmitter at his ear as he walked toward them. Two officers would cruise the block, looking for loiterers. Ryan Mills would pull the SUV up to the private entrance while Dave retrieved the Lincoln and brought it around to State Street.

Varying her routine was part of the plan to keep Jillian safe. But it was impossible to make mundane events truly random, and if the shooter kept trying, Dave knew that sooner or later, he might just get it right.

EIGHT

Jillian wondered if she would be safer with a detective sitting beside her, instead of both officers riding in the front, but then Senator Armstrong would have to sit with the driver, and that wouldn't go over well with him, she was sure. She settled back against the soft upholstery and smiled at her friend in the light of the street-lamps.

"Well, Joe, how have you been these past few weeks? I hope you're over that nasty cold you had after Christmas."

"Yes, I think I am, finally."

Jillian found herself watching the back of Dave's head and thinking what a handsome driver she had tonight. Penny was watching him, too, and she murmured something. Dave glanced over at his seatmate and answered quietly. Dave and Penny would make a cute couple.

The thought sent a pang of sadness through Jillian. Dave had demonstrated the integrity and diligence she valued. He was the first man who had attracted her since Brendon's death. But she couldn't contemplate a relationship with him, no matter how strong her feelings for him were.

It would be dangerous for both of them—possibly even disastrous.

In the warmth of the vehicle, she unbuttoned her coat. The Kevlar vests the detectives had insisted she and Joe wear were not overly uncomfortable.

"So what have you been up to lately?" she asked the senator.

Joe grinned at her. "I've stayed close to home so far this winter, but my kids all came to visit over the holidays. I've spoken a couple of times, but close by. Thomas College and Colby. Just informal talks about the Washington scene."

"Sounds like fun."

Penny turned around. "How are you doing, Governor? Anything we can do for you? I'm sure you know that you can close the partition if you want more privacy."

"We're fine, thanks." Jillian glanced over at Joe. "No secrets to discuss, are there?"

He laughed. "I'm way past that."

She continued to chat with her old friend, and after a while Penny and Dave struck up a quiet conversation in the front seat. Dave seemed intent on his driving and only commented now and then, but Penny grew more animated as the miles flew by.

The radio crackled now and then, and Penny responded. Outside, the velvety night sky twinkled. Jillian could see the taillights of the familiar

SUV ahead of them. As they approached Bangor, Dave slowed down. Twenty minutes later, he pulled up at a side door of the Maine Center for the Arts.

Andrew parked in a handicapped space nearby. He and Ryan jumped out and hurried to the Lincoln. Dave looked back at Jillian and the senator.

"All set?" he asked.

"I think so," Jillian replied.

"You've both got your body armor on?"

"Yes, confound it." Joe fumbled with the buttons on his overcoat. Jillian nodded.

"Okay, we'll open your doors at the same time. Go with the officers quickly into the hall. They'll get you directly up to the box. I'll see you in about an hour when Andrew and I switch duties."

They arrived in their seats about fifteen minutes before the program opened. Several people Jillian knew came to the door of the box and asked to speak to her. Penny scurried back and forth to tell her who had arrived, and Ryan admitted them a few at a time. Jillian felt Joe was as big an attraction as she was. He seemed better able to toss off witticisms and keep the guests laughing. Andrew and Penny graciously herded them out before the performance began, and Jillian sat down and caught her breath. She was glad she'd come. She glanced over at Joe. He winked at her and turned his attention to the orchestra.

She couldn't help but think about Dave, alone in the parking lot, and was pleased when he appeared at her elbow during the last number before the intermission. She always felt safer when Dave was next to her, but she knew that wasn't the only reason her spirits lifted.

During the intermission, Jillian was again deluged with people who wished to greet her. She had no time to sample the refreshments sent up to her box, though Joe somehow managed to snag a drink that she didn't think was iced tea. The maestro, on hearing that she would not be able to stay for the reception afterward, came up to thank her for coming and wish her well. Dave assured Jillian they had cleared him for security, though his name didn't appear on their original visitors list.

Jillian turned to greet the next arrivals, straining to hear what they said over the swell of voices. The box was getting crowded. She looked around for Dave and caught his eye. He arched his eyebrows and eased over next to Penny. Soon after, Penny moved among the visitors, gently urging them to step outside and allow others a brief chance to see the governor. Such a fuss, Jillian thought. Over who? Me?

Dave stood silently to one side for the most part, appraising each visitor. He looked frequently across the auditorium to the balconies and boxes opposite. Jillian supposed he was watching for suspicious movement in other parts of the hall. She was enjoying herself, but even so, she wished she were an ordinary concertgoer with no need for a security force of four and several local policemen all evening. And as fond as she'd grown of Joe Armstrong, she wished the dashing young detective stood at her side instead of the silver-haired senator.

Dave exited first, by the side door where they'd entered the concert hall. The subzero air smacked into him, but he left his hood down for maximum peripheral vision. Penny and Senator Armstrong lingered just inside, with Jillian and Ryan behind them. Penny waited for his signal, watching through the small glass window in the metal door. Dave crossed the frozen asphalt to where Andrew stood between the two official vehicles.

"All clear?" Dave asked.

"So far," Andrew replied. "It's too cold for much action out here."

Dave nodded and waved to Penny. She opened the door to bring the senator out. Andrew opened the door of the SUV, according to plan. Dave wanted to switch the governor and her guest from the Lincoln to the SUV for the ride home as one final break in routine to confuse anyone watching.

He scanned the parking lot. A few rows over, two people walked between the rows of vehicles. Closer, a man headed for the door, hunched against the cold. As Armstrong approached the vehicle and slid into the backseat, Dave unzipped his parka and slipped his hand inside, near his sidearm, just in case.

Penny headed back to the side door, so that she and Ryan could flank Jillian on her walk to the SUV. She reached the door half a dozen strides before the approaching man did.

Dave called out, "Sir!"

The man faltered and turned toward him. "Me? You talking to me?"

Penny slipped inside the building.

"Yes, sir." Dave held a hand up to the pedestrian. "I need to have you wait a minute before you go in."

The man scowled. "It's cold out here."

"Yes, sir. I apologize. Just wait here with me, please. This will only take a minute." Dave pulled out his badge and held it up in the beams of the streetlight above.

"Oh. Uh . . . I'm just here to pick up my wife."

Dave took his arm and pulled him back a few paces. Better to have him where Dave could watch him than to let him come face-to-face with the governor in the hallway. "Just stay right here. Don't move until I tell you."

"Okay." The man's knit hat came down over his eyebrows, but he kept his hands in his pockets and shivered as he watched the door.

Dave glanced back toward the SUV. Andrew lifted his hand, signaling him to proceed. Dave gave Penny and Ryan his signal, and the door opened.

Penny emerged first. Ryan held the door open for Jillian. After his first glimpse of her a sudden movement at Dave's side caught his attention. The man leaped out before him and faced the door. Penny was only two steps away, and her eyes widened as she jerked to a halt.

"Gun!"

As Penny yelled, Jillian nearly barreled into her.

Dave had only a nanosecond to decide—tackle or shoot. He whipped out his pistol. As though someone had slowed the action, he saw every movement clearly: Penny lunging backward to carry Jillian down, Ryan jumping toward the governor, Andrew racing for the man, and the pistol the interloper held, reflecting light from the streetlamps.

Dave's pistol cracked. A second shot echoed off the building. Andrew piled on top of the man, and Dave rushed to his aid.

"Get the governor in the car," he yelled to Penny.

She stared, white-faced, for an instant, then

turned to help Jillian to her feet. Ryan was already bending over her.

Dave picked up the pistol that had fallen from the shooter's hand. The 9 mm Glock's clip held six rounds of copper-jacketed bullets.

He whipped out his handcuffs. Andrew already had the prone man subdued.

"Go!" Dave yelled to Ryan. "Get her to the car. Quick!"

Andrew stood. "I don't think we need the cuffs. You got him."

"Call for an ambulance," Dave said.

Ten feet away, Jillian rose slowly, grasping Ryan's hand.

"Are you hurt, ma'am?" Ryan asked.

"My ankle."

"Are you shot?" Ryan asked.

Dave reached her in three strides.

"No." Jillian brushed back her hair. "I twisted it going down."

"It's probably my fault," Penny said, offering her hand to steady the governor. Jillian took a step and winced.

Dave touched her arm. "We need to get you away before the crowd comes out. Hold on." He bent his knees and lifted her, and she twined her arm around his neck. It was only a few steps to the SUV. Ryan dashed past him to open the door. Andrew already had a phone connection and was asking for backup.

Dave placed Jillian gently on the backseat next to Armstrong, not wanting to let her go. She looked up into his eyes. The fear he saw there nearly broke his heart.

"You okay?" Dave asked.

"Yes. Thank you."

He nodded. "We'll take you directly to a hospital. Eastern Maine Medical, I imagine, but Andrew will get orders. Buckle up. We're leaving."

"I heard a shot," Senator Armstrong quavered. "What happened?"

Jillian reached over to pat his hand. "It's all right, Joe. God protected us."

Dave shut the door and hurried to the driver's seat. Two uniformed officers came out the side door of the building and stopped, staring at the man on the pavement. Ryan headed over to them to help Penny.

"Go to EMMC," Andrew called to Dave. "Bangor police will meet you at the emergency entrance."

"Got it. Tell the colonel and the E.R. staff it's a twisted ankle, not a gunshot wound." Dave jumped into the SUV, buckled his seat belt and headed toward Bangor as people surged out of the building to see what happened. He was furious with himself for allowing the shooter anywhere near Jillian. She trusted him with her life, and this was how he repaid her?

If anything had happened to her, he never would have forgiven himself—ever. Was it possible that his feelings were getting in the way of his ability to do his job?

NINE

Dave drove in silence as they merged onto the interstate, trying not to convey his fury.

"Please don't take me to the hospital." Jillian sat forward and leaned on the back of the front seat.

Dave looked at her in the rearview mirror. "You need to have your ankle checked."

"It's not serious. I'll ice it when we get home. Besides, if we go to EMMC, we'll be there a couple of hours. You know we will. And there's only one of you to protect me now."

She was right about the extra time at the hospital, though Dave was sure the staff would expedite the governor's visit. But security would be tricky, even with the Bangor P.D. on alert.

"We could have your personal physician meet us at the Blaine House," Dave said.

Jillian frowned. "I'd hate to get her out so late. It's after nine o'clock now. It'll be eleven before we reach Augusta, won't it?"

Dave glanced at the dashboard clock. "Nearly. But you've got to see a doctor tonight. That's imperative. If it's worse than you think—"

"Okay. Put the word out for Dr. St. Pierre." She settled back beside the senator.

"Are you sure, Jillian?" Armstrong asked. "I don't mind going to the hospital with you."

Dave noted the strain in the old man's voice. Taking Joe Armstrong with them to another public place could pose problems, especially if he was upset.

"I'd rather go home and see my own doctor," Jillian said calmly. "Besides, this will get you home before midnight. If we stopped at the hospital, who knows when we'd get to bed?"

Dave fished out his cell phone and punched in the colonel's emergency line.

"Hutchins! Where are you? More to the point, where's Bronte?"

Dave almost smiled, in spite of the circumstances. Before the inauguration, Stephanie Drake had suggested the code name for the governor at one of their unit briefings. "Charlotte Bronte wrote Jane Eyre, and Jane was a governess." Stephanie was dead serious when she said it, but everyone in the briefing room had cracked up. The code name stuck.

"We're on I-95 and heading straight to Augusta. Could you please inform the Bangor police and Eastern Maine Medical that we're not stopping? The passenger prefers her own physician."

"Browne says she's not seriously injured."

"No, just a twisted ankle."

"Is Armstrong with you?"

Dave winced. The officers were supposed to

use a code name for the senator, as well, but you couldn't correct the colonel on something like that.

"Yes, sir. All's well with him."

"All right. We'll contact Bangor P.D. and the hospital," Smith said.

"Thank you. And if you could give the doctor a ring and see if she's available for a house call this evening . . ."

"Will do."

Dave closed his phone, dropped it into the cup holder and was silent for the rest of the drive.

Stephanie Drake was waiting at the Blaine House when they arrived an hour and a half later, to act as Jillian's personal guard for the night. Three other EPU officers and four state troopers had also turned out to ensure Jillian's safe return.

Dave leaped out of the SUV and pushed past Bob Caruthers to get to Jillian's door. He helped her out and bent to pick her up.

"I can walk," Jillian said with a laugh.

Dave merely glanced at her, making it clear that she would not be walking anywhere on his watch.

She gave in, and the officers surrounded Dave as he lifted her and quickly took her in through the family entrance and down the hall to the sun-room. He couldn't help but notice how it felt to have her arms entwined around his neck as he carried her, and it took all the strength he had not to look into her eyes. He gently put her down on the sofa, where Dr. St. Pierre was already waiting for her.

The doctor bent over her, gently probing her ankle. Stephanie sat close to Jillian, holding the governor's purse and bulletproof vest. Another EPU member, Tom Rawls, stood unobtrusively at the other hall door to the room.

"Where did the senator go?" Dave asked.

Bob nodded to the doorway across the hall. "In the family dining room, having a drink."

Dave arched his eyebrows.

"High-test coffee laced with cooking sherry," Bob said.

Apparently, the senator had gotten around Jillian's prohibition rules. "Is he driving himself home?"

"I can take him."

"Probably a good idea," Dave said. "Have another officer go along to deliver his car and ride back with you."

"Sure. I think he wants to wait until the doctor gives the official word that the governor's all right," Bob said.

Jillian sat up, fumbling with her evening shoes. With Stephanie and the doctor supporting her, she stood and hobbled toward him.

"Let's ice that right away," Dr. St. Pierre said, looking at Stephanie.

"Yes, ma'am. I'll get an ice bag and take it upstairs immediately."

"And you need to stay off it, Governor. I'm not sure I want you walking up those stairs."

Dave stepped forward. Jillian's pale face went a becoming shade of rose. "I'd like to say goodnight to Senator Armstrong. He hasn't left, has he?"

"No, ma'am. Bob Caruthers will take him home after you've seen him."

Bob hurried across to the dining room, and a moment later Joe appeared with him in the doorway.

"What's the verdict, Doctor?" he boomed.

Dr. St. Pierre smiled at him. "I think the governor's assessment was accurate. It's not serious, but she needs to elevate it, ice it, and rest for a couple of days."

"Joe, thank you so much for going with me tonight." Jillian held out her hands to him and he grasped them.

"I enjoyed it right up until the finale."

"Me too. Did you get your coffee?" Jillian glanced anxiously at Bob.

"Yes, I did. And now you need your rest."

"I do apologize for the way the evening ended. Will you call me tomorrow?"

Joe's eyes softened as he patted her hands. "Of course. I'll want to know how you're doing."

"I'll expect your call," Jillian said. She turned

to Dave and held up her hand before he could approach her. "I think I've been carried enough for one night. Stephanie, will you help me walk up the stairs? I'm sure I can manage. Thank you, everyone, for your help tonight. Perhaps this nightmare is finally over."

Dave watched as Jillian made her way slowly up the stairs, still able to feel her in his arms, the warmth of her against him.

Dave caught only a few hours of restless sleep. He rose early and shaved, ignoring the dark circles under his eyes. At EPU headquarters, he filed his report, then read those submitted by the other officers at the scene of the shooting.

Lieutenant Wilson came in shortly after seven. The fact that he was in the office on a Sunday morning underscored the gravity of the situation.

"Good job last night, Hutchins." Wilson clapped him on the shoulder. "Has the *Today Show* called you yet?"

Dave stared up at him, speechless, aware that he probably looked as savvy as a half-witted raccoon.

Wilson laughed. "You're a hero. The receptionist just told me she's getting a gazillion calls from the media."

Dave gritted his teeth. He certainly didn't feel like a hero. "I won't have to do a press conference, will I?"

"We'll let Mark Payson handle it. But it wouldn't surprise me if all the networks sent camera crews here to interview you."

"I'll be in the field, doing my job."

Wilson shrugged. "Hey, a little good publicity wouldn't hurt the unit any. But we'll try to keep them off your back."

"Will I be suspended?"

"It's customary to give an officer leave after a shooting, until the investigation is complete."

"I need to be working on this, sir."

"I'll speak to the colonel," Wilson said. "The governor's requested to see you this afternoon."

Dave's stomach did a little flip. "At the Blaine House?"

"Yes. Gutsy woman. She insists on going to her statehouse office tomorrow. And she says the ankle's only giving her a few twinges this morning."

"Good. I see we've ID'd the shooter. She'll have a lot of questions, though."

"Like 'Why?'"

"Yes," Dave said, "and whether he acted alone."

Wilson frowned. "Well, he can't tell us that now."

To Dave's surprise, Jillian was in the sunroom when he arrived at four in the afternoon. She was seated at the piano playing softly, wearing a long-sleeved ivory top and a print skirt. Stephanie sat near the windows. Dave paused in the doorway, listening. Beethoven, if he wasn't mistaken. He watched her hands glide skillfully over the keys. The governor was good, no question about that.

When the melody wound down in a quiet finale, Dave and Stephanie both applauded.

Jillian rose, flushing a bit and smiling apologetically. "I've wanted to try this piano for the past month, and never found a moment when there was no one around. Not that you two are 'no one.'" Her blush deepened. "I guess the concert last night got to me."

"That was wonderful." Stephanie stood and stepped forward. "I had no idea you could play."

Jillian tossed her head. "Mom made me practice way after I wanted to stop. She was very disappointed when I quit after high school."

"You should play more often," Dave said. Her playing had warmed his heart even more than the stirring orchestral music they'd heard the evening before.

"You two are sworn to silence." Jillian glared at them both, but her eyes twinkled. "It's a state secret. I don't want to be railroaded into playing at some function or other."

Dave was glad she could tease them, glad that her thoughts weren't mired in the tragedy of the shooting.

"Naomi must know what a good pianist you

are," Stephanie mused. "She never said a word, though."

"Oh, yes. She came to our house after school every day for years, until her mom got off work, and she heard me suffer through practice every afternoon. She hated it as much as I did, I think. It meant we couldn't play or ride bikes until I was finished." Jillian carefully closed the keyboard.

"Naomi Plante was in your class, wasn't she?" Dave tried to recall what he'd read in her background file.

Jillian nodded. "Her mom was a single parent, and she made an after-school child care arrangement with my mother that lasted about five years."

"You must have grown close," Stephanie said.

Jillian shrugged. "Somewhat. We're alike in a lot of ways, and yet we're very different. But we've stayed friends for all this time."

Stephanie smiled. "Well, I know you have business to discuss. Your mother should be here soon. I'll make rounds through the family quarters before she and Naomi get here. Would you like coffee? I can put in a request for you."

Jillian arched her eyebrows at Dave. "How about it? I think I'd like a cup."

"Sure," he said.

"In my office upstairs, please," Jillian told Stephanie, who nodded and left the room.

"How's the ankle?" Dave asked.

"Not bad. If not for the circumstances last night, I probably would have ignored it." They went into the hallway and walked to the staircase. "Did you get to church today?" she asked.

"Yes." He'd gone to church that morning after filing his report, and the service had calmed him somewhat, but he'd slipped out during the final prayer to avoid people's questions. "I guess you were kept busy here."

She made a face. "Yes. This morning the doctor came by again, then the department spokesman and Colonel Smith. But next week I'm going to church for sure. I want my routine back."

"I hope you can have it."

"Colonel Smith gave me the lowdown this morning, but I suppose the unit has been busy all day."

"Yes," Dave said. "Every member but me."

"Oh. Why is that?"

In the upper hallway, he opened the office door for her and followed her inside. "It's standard procedure. I'm officially off duty until the case is reviewed."

She pulled over one of the comfortable leather chairs. Dave hung his jacket on the back of his, and they sat down next to each other.

"You killed the man," she said, "but everyone knows you did it for me. You were doing your job, I mean."

"Yes. The colonel assures me I have nothing to

worry about. The review is a formality. It makes you a little nervous, though, until the internal investigation is over."

Even now, thinking about those few seconds when he'd realized the man intended to kill Jillian sent a tremor through him.

"Jillian, I owe you an apology. That man should never have been anywhere near you."

"You saved my life, Dave." She gazed intently into his eyes. "I want to thank you for that, but words seem so inadequate."

He swallowed hard. "I'm glad I was there, but still, I—"

She shook her and mustered a smile. "I've thanked God all day long. Andrew was magnificent, too, leaping on him like he did. I'm afraid either Penny or I would have been shot if you hadn't acted precisely when you did."

Dave thought, as he had a thousand times in the last eighteen hours, that he should have frisked the man before he let Jillian leave the concert hall.

"I'm happy to report that we got a match on the gun he used last night. Our ballistics lab says its bullets match the slug from the inauguration day shooting."

Jillian caught her breath. "You're sure?"

"Absolutely. This is the same gun."

She exhaled. "Thank God. That's one answer, at least."

A soft tap on the door preceded Beth's entry.

"Here's the coffee, ma'am." She set the tray on the desk before them.

"Thank you, Beth. Has my mother arrived yet?" Jillian asked.

"No, ma'am."

Jillian turned to Dave. "I've persuaded Mom to spend a couple of days with me again."

When Beth left the room, Dave said, "I'm glad Mrs. Clark's coming, but you do understand that we can't go lax on your security?"

"Oh, of course not." Jillian reached for her mug. "But things should be a little less tense now, shouldn't they?"

"A bit. But we still don't know much about the second shooting. We're hoping to find something in the shooter's residence. Did the colonel tell you who the man was?"

"Yes. Wesley Stevenson. I can't say I recall hearing the name before, but it's a fairly common one. Colonel Smith said the EPU will do a complete investigation into his background."

"It may take several days before we get a conclusive report. Carl Millbridge is checking to see if Stevenson had crossed your legal path in the past. At this point we don't think he showed up as a defendant in any of your court cases."

"That's good, I suppose. But it might be better if we knew he had a reason to hate me."

Dave took a sip of coffee to stop himself from

saying that he found it impossible to believe anyone could hate her, despite evidence to the contrary.

She frowned. "I wish we could know for certain that it was the same man—I mean, that it was Wesley Stevenson all three times."

Dave would certainly sleep better if they knew that. A lot of people would. But he said nothing.

"When will you be able to resume work?" she asked.

"Maybe as soon as Wednesday."

"So you get a couple of days off to relax and enjoy yourself."

He chuckled. "I'm not sure how much relaxing I'll be able to do."

She sipped her coffee, then looked at him. "What do you do for fun anyway? I know you're dead serious about your job. All of you EPU officers are alike in that way. Won't let me out in the yard alone for half a minute. But you must have hobbies when you're off duty."

He studied her for a moment. She'd deliberately taken the conversation out of official territory. Was that significant, or did she simply not want to discuss the dead man anymore? "I like to read. And I hunt. In summer, I do some canoeing."

"Oh, I love canoeing." She held her mug with both hands and smiled. "Where's your favorite spot?"

"Kennebago River, I guess."

"I like lakes better than rivers for canoeing," she said. "I'm not skillful enough for white water."

"I like a good river run now and then, but a nice, calm lake is better."

Jillian leaned with one elbow on the desk. "Brendon and I went up to Moosehead for two weeks the summer before he died." Her smile tilted a little.

Dave could see the pain in her eyes and wished he could ease it somehow. "I used to go with my brother."

She perked up immediately. "Oh, you have a brother. Older or younger?"

"Younger. And a sister. She lives at home still. She's twenty—going to UMA."

"And your brother?"

Dave inhaled deeply. "He's in Iraq."

She stared at him for a moment, her face troubled. "You were in Iraq, too. Someone told me that."

He nodded. "Two tours."

"It must be hard to see your little brother go."

"Yeah." He reminded himself that the odds were good Matt would come back in fine shape. "I'm proud of him." Despite his efforts, his voice cracked. He remembered his first combat experience. If he could spare Matt that, he would do anything in his power. Taking down the man who wanted to kill Jillian last night had been easy compared to seeing his friends fall in combat.

Jillian reached over and touched his hand for an instant, then drew back. "Would you mind if I prayed for him?"

"Not a bit. In fact, Matt and I would both appreciate that. Thanks."

"Dave . . ."

As he looked up to meet her pensive gaze, another soft knock came at the door.

"Come in." Jillian looked expectantly toward the sound.

Stephanie entered, smiling. "Your mother is here, Governor. She's in her room, getting settled."

Dave rose, picked up his jacket and slipped it on. "Have a good evening. Thanks for the coffee."

Jillian's smile soothed the ache in his heart. The people of Maine, more than a million strong, vied for her attention. Tonight, for fifteen minutes, he'd had her all to himself.

"Dave, thank you for everything." She stood and took his hand in both hers for a moment. His heart thundered as he gazed down into her eyes.

"I'm glad you're all right," he said. "Have a good night's rest."

"I think I will. And I'll pray that you're back on active duty soon."

"Thank you." He stood too long, looking down at her. If he'd acted a moment too late . . . but he hadn't. She was safe. And others would watch over her until he was allowed back. Which couldn't happen a moment too soon.

TEN

When Jillian answered her phone on Thursday afternoon, Lettie's words set her pulse racing.

"Detective Hutchins is here, Governor. He has some news for you on the Stevenson investigation. If you can give him a few minutes, he'd like to see you."

"Of course. Oh, Lettie, I have someone coming at three . . ."

"I believe they just entered the outer office. I'll seat them until you're finished with the detective."

Jillian sat back and took a deep breath. Every time she'd thought about Dave lately, she'd tried to convince herself that her feelings for him were illogical and temporary. But careful consideration brought the opposite conclusion. What could be more logical than falling for the man who had done so much to protect her? This was more than an adolescent crush. She admired and appreciated Dave's diligence, his sympathy and kindness, and she found herself wishing their relationship could transcend business and become something more personal . . . and more permanent.

He entered, smiling, and she stood to shake his hand.

"Dave! You're back at work."

"Who told you?"

"You did. I can tell by the satisfaction on your face."

He laughed. "I admit being on leave depressed me. It feels good to be back on the job."

"You look great." She immediately wondered if the remark was too personal, but his dark gray suit, pearl-gray shirt and burgundy necktie, along with his dashing good looks, put him in the head-turning category.

"Thanks. I feel great. How about you? Any pain in that ankle?"

"No, it's fine. What can you tell me today?"

He sat down opposite her, and sobered as he looked into her eyes for a long moment. "We've found a connection between you and Stevenson."

She caught her breath. "What?"

"Roderick Tanger."

"He's still in prison."

"Yes." Between Dave's eyebrows, little vertical lines spelled regret and concern.

"It's all right," she said. "Tell me everything you know."

"Okay. This Wesley Stevenson—the gunman—worked for Tanger."

"Before Tanger was convicted?"

"Yes. And some say he still did."

Jillian studied his face. "You think Tanger's still running his so-called business from the Maine State Prison?"

"Maybe. Other men are doing the legwork—bringing the drugs in, collecting the payments. But Tanger may still have a hand in it. We've got three detectives in Portland and another at the prison right now, trying to ferret out information."

"So you think Tanger is carrying out the revenge he's wanted on me for nearly a decade?"

"I think it's possible. We're looking into Stevenson's connections now and trying to determine how he's supported himself recently. The car he drove to Orono Saturday night wasn't flashy enough to draw attention, but it's not a cheap model. The detectives in Portland searched his house, and they tell us he lived pretty well. We're looking at his bank records now."

She nodded slowly. "Anything else?"

"Yes. They found a rifle. The lab will test it. They should be able to tell if it fired the round from the parking garage."

"That would be progress."

"The thing is, Tanger's been a model prisoner. If he's still running drugs, we have no proof. And the prison is crowded. They want his room."

"You're not serious," Jillian said, her stomach suddenly in knots.

"He'll have a parole hearing this summer."

She frowned and looked down at her desk, gathering a few stray papers and nervously tapping them into a neat stack. "I can recommend that the parole board refuses to release him."

"Maybe you should set up a meeting with the attorney general."

"I'll ask. But if they can't find any evidence . . ." She jotted "Call the AG" on a slip of memo paper, then looked up into Dave's brown eyes. "You seriously think Roderick Tanger was behind these attacks."

"I don't know. But it's the best lead we've had in a long time."

They sat for half a minute without speaking. Jillian remembered Tanger's fury when the verdict came down at his trial. She shivered, and despised her own weakness.

"Thank you," she said at last. "I know this is your job, but it's more than that to me."

"I know," he said softly. "I wish I could make it go away. If we find anything that shows Tanger was communicating with Stevenson, we'll throw away the key on him. But if he had nothing to do with it . . ."

She nodded. "I'd be the last one to want an innocent man punished for this. Thank you for everything. I feel as though it's more than a challenge for you. That you really care, not only on the professional level, but . . ."

"I do. I care very much."

Jillian's pulse quickened at his husky tone and the warmth in his eyes. She warned herself not to make too much of it, but she felt an unexpected wave of happiness. They gazed at each other across the desk. There were so many things she wished they could say, but she wouldn't break protocol, and neither would he.

With reluctance, she pulled her gaze away. Her three o'clock appointment had been waiting ten minutes.

Before she could speak, Dave rose.

"It's been a pleasure, Governor. I'll keep you posted on our findings."

That Sunday, Jillian felt more optimistic than she had in weeks. She and Naomi rode to her hometown to attend services at her own church, a welcome change from the cloistered existence she'd lived for nearly two months. The pastor's sermon reminded her that God was in control of everything—the investigation, the workings of the state and, yes, even her personal life.

Jillian's mother, who had returned to her own house the day before, met her and Naomi in the auditorium before the worship service. She insisted that the two EPU officers with them, Penny and Ryan, join them for lunch at her home afterward. On the return drive to Augusta, with Penny at the wheel of the SUV, Jillian talked quietly with Naomi.

"I meant to tell you," Naomi said, "I have a date for Friday evening."

"Oh?" Jillian asked. "Someone new?" She couldn't recall Naomi dating anyone since they'd moved to Augusta.

Naomi chuckled. "It's Beth's cousin."

Jillian stared at her. "Beth? You mean our Beth?"

"Yes, the one who helps Amelia in the kitchen. He's going to be in town next weekend, and Beth wanted to line up someone for a foursome with her and her boyfriend."

"That could be interesting," Jillian said.

"She warned me that he's an accountant, and he never reads anything but science fiction."

Jillian laughed. "You hate sci-fi. And you always came crying to me for help with your math."

"I know." Naomi grimaced. "But Beth is fun. It'll be something different."

"You'll have to tell me how it goes." Jillian leaned back and closed her eyes. She was glad Naomi had made friends with Beth. It made Jillian feel less guilty about how unavailable she'd been lately, as a friend.

She let her mind roam. Since Stevenson's shooting, she'd done two press conferences. The first, on Monday, had included reporters from the networks, as well as Maine newspapers and TV stations. The second, held Friday morning in the Hall of Flags, was limited to in-state journalists, though some of the networks had run clips on their evening broadcasts. Jillian preferred to let Mark Payson do the interviews, but she saw the wisdom of letting the world see her unscathed face after the nearly successful assassination attempt.

Her short interludes with Dave Hutchins brought more pleasant memories. Those few minutes alone with him at the mansion and in her statehouse office had sown a seed of longing she didn't think she'd ever feel again. Ten years ago, she and Brendon had planned their life, their home and their family together. Did she still have a chance at that? Was there still time for her to have children and a family life?

Not without a husband.

But she'd signed on for four years in a very high-stress job. This was not the time to think of dating or marrying or becoming a mother, much as she yearned for those things. Yet, when she thought of Dave, the longing pierced her deeply.

She let out a sigh.

"You okay?" Naomi asked.

"Yeah. Sorry. Just thinking."

"Is your mom coming to stay with us again soon?"

"I hope so." Jillian opened her eyes.

"I was going to spend next weekend with my mother, but now that I have a date . . ."

"You can always go home on Saturday," Jillian said.

"Maybe. We'll see. We've been so busy since the inauguration that I haven't been home much," Naomi said. "I should go soon."

"Yes, you should."

Jillian closed her eyes again, mulling over her new life. At first she'd found the domestic staff and security officers annoying. No matter where she went, someone was only steps away. It rankled her independent soul. Since becoming a widow, she'd done things for herself and enjoyed her privacy and solitude. But she'd lost that now. A simple walk in the park required complicated schedule shuffling and arrangements for her security.

But if she expected to stay alive and maintain a semblance of a normal life, the EPU was necessary. And Dave Hutchins was more than necessary. She had absolutely no idea what she was going to do about that.

Dave tapped his fingers on the edge of his keyboard and scowled at the spreadsheet on the screen. More than a week had passed since he'd shot the stalker. They were still investigating the dead man, probing Stevenson's associates and his connection to Roderick Tanger. Dave had made two trips to southern Maine to interview people who had known the dead man after Carl

Millbridge parceled out the interviews to several detectives. Dave was getting to the end of his lengthy list. He closed his eyes for a moment and sent up a silent prayer. *Lord, help us to not overlook something critical.*

He would see Jillian tonight, having resumed the biweekly briefings in her office at the Blaine House. He tried to ignore how much he was looking forward to seeing her.

He was still at the computer when the lieutenant called him at quarter to six.

"The governor is working late at the statehouse. Detectives Mills and Thurlow are scheduled to take her home, but Mills's shift ends in a few minutes. If you're available, the governor thought it might be easiest if you update her at the statehouse. Help Thurlow get her home, and Bob Caruthers will take over for you at the Blaine House."

"Sounds good," Dave said, thinking he'd rather meet with Jillian in the office at the mansion. It felt more private.

He drove to the huge parking lot outside the state office building. Most of the workers had left for the day. He walked around the massive utilitarian building that ruined the view of the statehouse from most nearby vantage points.

As he rounded the corner, he surveyed the back of the Capitol building, from the open area where Jillian had given her ill-fated press conference on inauguration day, to the copper-covered dome topped with a statue of Wisdom. As always, the sight stirred him.

He crossed the lobby, bypassed the elevator and took the broad marble staircase instead, coming up into the majestic Hall of Flags on the second floor. The entrance to the governor's office was tucked away, with a sign so small beside the door that it would be easy to miss. The EPU officer standing on duty outside indicated Jillian's presence in the chambers. The receptionist had left for the night, and her small office was empty. Dave swung to the right into the next, much larger room.

In the spacious outer office, Jillian's administrative assistant, Lettie Wheeler, was pulling on her coat. Dave knew little about her, but she always had a smile and a kind word for the officers.

"The governor is expecting you," she told him. "I'm heading out, but when you are finished, the two officers on duty here will help the governor lock up and see her home."

"Actually, I'm one of the two who will escort her tonight," Dave said. "Things must be busy around here."

Lettie nodded. "You could say that. Governor Goff has been meeting with legislators and lobbyists all day. She's determined to see that tax bill go down, but there are a lot of people who would like to see it pass. If you want my advice, keep the briefing short and take her home to get some rest." She winked at him, and Dave chuckled.

"I'll keep that in mind. Thank you."

Lettie leaned over her desk and pushed a button on the phone. "Detective Hutchins is here."

"Thanks, Lettie," Jillian's clear voice said. "Good night."

Dave watched the older woman leave and turned toward the closed oak door of the inner office. He tapped on the panel, and the door opened from inside. Another officer greeted him and stepped outside, allowing Dave to enter, and closed the door behind him.

"Dave." Jillian waved him in.

He took a seat and smiled down at her. "Long day?"

"Yes, but I think I made a lot of progress on a couple of fronts today."

"Energy and taxes?"

"My, you are keeping up with the statehouse scuttlebutt, aren't you?"

He laughed, slightly embarrassed. She grinned at him.

"I suppose we could have waited and had our talk at the Blaine House, as usual." She sat back in her chair. "I'm about done here for tonight, but if I went over now, there would barely be time between when we got there and dinner. I wouldn't want to be rude to the chef, but I'd hate to make you wait. I don't suppose you'd sit down to dinner with Naomi and me?"

Dave gritted his teeth. "Thank you, but I'm sure there's some rule or other against that."

"Thought so." Jillian crossed her legs and smiled. "So. Where are we in the investigation?"

"I have a list of eight people I'm looking hard at. I intend to interview all of them again within the next week."

"People I know?"

"Some." He took a slip of paper from his jacket pocket and passed it to her. "Half of them are people who worked with Tanger before he was incarcerated."

"Who else?" She looked down at the list, frowning. Dave took the opportunity to stare without reproach. She was beautiful, even if she didn't look happy. He realized that she'd started talking, and he wasn't listening.

"I can understand why you think Raymond Grant might have it in for me. He's a dedicated lobbyist, and I've butted heads with him many times—including this afternoon—over the petroleum issue."

"Grant has a lot riding on what happens during your administration. If the study you're pushing for leads you and your advisors to believe that drilling in the Gulf of Maine would be inadvisable—"

"For environmental reasons," she put in.

"For whatever reasons. That would cost Raymond Grant a bundle. He's banking on getting a green flag to drill."

"He knows we have to consider all the possibilities. I'm not against drilling for oil here, if we can do it safely. But I don't think the federal government will let us move in that direction, even if we find that it would benefit the people of Maine in every conceivable way. And if it's found to be risky . . ."

"Grant knows all that. But if he'd seen someone elected who was gung ho on the project, his stock would have climbed. He and his colleagues are pressuring you to hurry up that study, aren't they?"

She put one hand to her forehead and sighed. "Somewhat." She looked back down at the list. "I thought you'd ruled out Parker Tilton."

"He's still first in line to be governor if anything happens to you. We haven't found a solid motive other than that, but we can't totally exclude him from the equation. Ditto for your opponent in the election, Peter Harrison."

She stood and paced to the tall window, where she looked down at the grounds and street below. Dave resisted the instinct to tell her not to stand in the window like that.

At last she turned and came back to her chair. "Why are we still looking at these people?"

"You know why."

She exhaled heavily. "We can't prove Stevenson acted alone. We can't prove he fired at me from the parking garage—yet. But if someone hired him—and even if there was more than one gunman in the three shooting attempts—isn't the connection to Roderick Tanger strong enough?"

"No. I'm sorry. We haven't found any communication between the two of them since Tanger went to jail."

"Who's running his business now?"

"His old network seems to have splintered. Those first four names are people who worked for him. They all have other connections now, some legal and some not. We're investigating very thoroughly, and some of them may face unrelated criminal charges. But Tanger seems to be a drone now that he's behind bars. The corrections system may have successfully isolated him from his former contacts."

"How can we know that for sure?" she asked. "Aren't there always leaks?"

Dave didn't like her thinking, but she was right. "We can't know everything. I'm praying hard that if there's something there, we'll find it, so the case will break and we can assure you that you're safe."

"Can I stop wearing a bulletproof vest every

time I go out now? I wore one to the opening of a new elementary school yesterday, for crying out loud!"

"I'm sorry that was necessary."

"I know you're frustrated, too. Can't we just trust God that this is over and act normal?" she asked.

"That would be great. But if we were wrong . . ."

Jillian raised her chin. "I pray for the same thing over and over. 'Let the EPU guys find something, Lord! Give us proof that this Stevenson was a crazy who resented me for putting his boss in the slammer.'"

"God doesn't always answer our prayers in the way or in the time frame that we think is best."

"I know. Yes, I know that's true." She lowered her forehead into her hands and closed her eyes. "If he wasn't in touch with Tanger, why would he care about me?"

"Another option I've considered is that Stevenson had a new boss after Tanger was put away. Someone else who resented you. He might be doing the same line of work he did for Tanger, but for someone else."

"But we don't know who."

Dave glanced around, wondering if anyone was watching them on the closed-circuit cameras. "Is it . . . truly private in here?"

"Yes. If you mean is our conversation being recorded, it's not."

He eyed her cautiously for a long moment. When she met his gaze again, he asked softly, "Would it be all right if we prayed about this together?"

"I . . ." She sat still, looking into his eyes. Gradually her lips slipped into a weary smile. "Yes. I'd like that very much."

He reached across her desk and took her hands in his, and bowed his head.

ELEVEN

Hey, Hutchins, wait up."

Dave paused and let the other officers pass him, emptying the duty room after the Wednesday-morning briefing. Carl Millbridge hung back, glaring stonily at him.

Dave waited just inside the doorway, wishing at least one other officer had lingered behind.

"What's up, Carl?"

"You've been going over all the interviews I did in the governor's case since inauguration day."

"That's right." Dave leaned back against the door frame. "I figured I'd read through all the data we've collected again. Is there a problem?"

"Not really. But I can tell you, there's nothing there."

Dave shrugged, not sure where Millbridge was going with this. "It can't hurt to go over what we have and see if we missed anything."

Carl gave him a long, dark look. "I didn't miss anything."

"Probably not. But it will help me get a fuller picture if I read other people's reports again. Not just yours. I aim to read through everybody's until I either find something to pursue or we get some new leads. We need to be aggressive on this case."

"What, you think I haven't been aggressive enough?"

"I didn't say that. But I'd have thought we could have had the ballistics report back on Stevenson's rifle in less than ten days."

"The lab was backlogged. Someone had vacation last week."

"So? I could have run a few rounds through that gun myself and checked the slugs. So could you. An hour tops, and we'd have known. This is our most important case ever, and we're waiting for some tech to get back from vacation?"

"Well, we know now, don't we?" Carl leaned toward Dave, his face a deep red.

At that moment, Lieutenant Wilson breezed through the doorway, almost smacking into Dave, who stepped quickly to one side.

Wilson stopped and looked back and forth between them.

"What's going on here?"

"Nothing," Carl said.

Wilson eyed him dubiously.

"Just discussing the fact that the rifle from Stevenson's apartment was the same one used on top of the parking garage at the end of January," Dave said.

"Yes. That's the good news and the bad, isn't it?" Wilson said.

Dave nodded. "It ties it up almost too neatly."

"You're just mad because there's no one left for you to chase," Carl muttered.

"No. I'm skeptical because, so far as we can tell, Stevenson had no motive. With the bits and pieces we've put together, I'm saying it was money, and that means someone was paying him. But who?"

"A lot of people are working on that," Wilson said. "The only people who've visited Tanger in prison for the last six months are his lawyer and his sister. I wish we could say it's over and close the file." He sighed. "You'll have to call Payson and brief him for a press conference today, Millbridge."

Dave still wondered if they'd pushed hard enough. He had to tread carefully, though. If he seemed too eager, someone might suspect he was developing personal feelings for the governor, and he would lose his job. He strived to keep his relationship with her strictly by-the-book, but he knew he was losing his heart. And if he were really honest with himself, he'd say he'd already lost it.

As for Carl, Dave had seen a tendency in him to hog the glory for the unit's successes, but accept none of the blame for their lack of results. Only a few days ago, Wilson had called Dave into his office and asked him some hard questions about the investigation. The lieutenant's probing had prompted Dave to hope Wilson would remove

Carl from the lead position in the investigation. So far he hadn't hinted at such a course.

But Dave was still the one briefing the governor twice a week. He'd gotten the assignment by default that first day—the two more senior investigating officers had gone off duty before the governor was free for a meeting. Somehow, he'd hung on to the duty. He hadn't asked why, for fear the responsibility would be passed to Carl and he would no longer see Jillian regularly.

Those briefings were Dave's only contact with her. He didn't want to lose that. He couldn't.

Jillian both loved and hated public hearings. They were a good way to get information to and from the people. Anyone could attend and ask questions of the lawmakers before they passed new legislation. However, when a controversial topic drew a large crowd and the question-and-answer time got out of hand, a hearing could turn into a free-for-all.

The bill under consideration today, which would fund large-scale alternative energy studies, threatened to be one of the noisy ones, where extra security was needed.

"I'm not sure you should go in there," Andrew Browne said Friday morning in her office. "There's a big crowd downstairs, and we've moved them to a larger room. The chairman is having a hard time quieting them down."

"It's a subject everyone has an opinion about," Jillian noted. "But it's also one I campaigned on vigorously. I promised my constituents that we'd take a fair look at all the options. I owe it to them to show up and confirm that we'll go forward with these studies. Maine needs to become more energy independent, and I'm not giving up on this because some people disagree with me."

"All right, if you insist."

"Andrew, I'm not trying to make your job more difficult. However, I need to live up to my promises."

"I understand."

They stepped into the outer office. Lettie stood and walked over to her.

"Chin up, my dear. Stick to what you've planned to say, and you'll be fine."

A uniformed officer joined them as they left the office. He took up a position outside the hearing room. Detective Stephanie Drake was waiting to accompany Jillian and Andrew inside.

A hush fell over the room as the Utilities and Energy Committee's chairman, Louis Moore, introduced her. Jillian was glad he would moderate the meeting. He always kept things moving and knew procedure inside out. She tried to project confidence as she strode to the lectern. Moore stood back, holding his ceremonial gavel with both hands.

"Welcome, Governor."

"Thank you, Senator Moore." Jillian turned to face the audience and was glad to see Dave slip in the side door halfway back. His presence always calmed her. "Thank you all for turning out on such a brutally cold day."

A slight ripple of laughter spread through the first few rows. She didn't see many faces she recognized, other than the small contingent from the press, a couple of lobbyists and the committee members.

She launched into her prepared statement about the need for low-cost and environmentally friendly energy.

"In addition, I want to see the exploration for oil go ahead in Maine waters," she concluded. "The required safety measures would make this doable, without the threat of disaster. We want to contain our energy costs and bring more jobs to Maine."

Sporadic clapping began, but a murmuring overrode it. Jillian moved aside and let Moore speak into the microphone.

"The governor has graciously agreed to take a few questions. Her tight schedule won't allow more, so keep your queries brief." He called on a reporter from the local newspaper, the *Kennebec Journal.*

"Governor, would you advocate the return of nuclear power plants to Maine if the federal government approved it?" the woman asked.

"I don't see this as an option any time in the near future, so it's not high on my list of energy alternatives," Jillian explained. "As you know, the Maine Yankee plant closed in 1996, and we haven't had a nuclear energy presence in Maine since. Other sources of energy are much less expensive and less controversial, although nuclear plants are safer now than they were in the past. If the economic situation changed and the option arose, I would ask the people of Maine whether or not they wanted to go that route again."

She glanced at Dave, but he wasn't watching her. Instead, he was watching the crowd. Jillian cast aside her mild disappointment. He was doing his job, and looking at her wouldn't keep her safe.

The moderator called on a man Jillian didn't recognize, but he carried a notebook and wore a sport jacket and tie, which led her to assume he was a journalist.

"Governor, what makes you think drilling for oil in the Gulf of Maine won't ruin our eco-system?"

The murmuring swelled. Jillian couldn't tell if the crowd disliked his question or her stance on the issue.

Moore leaned toward the microphone. "Folks, let's settle down and let the governor speak, please."

She looked out over the packed room. At least two hundred people had squeezed in, and the air felt close. Everyone waited for her answer. "As I've said before, I'm in favor of exploring any economically viable sources of energy. I've done a great deal of research on this topic, and I've talked to people who are experts in petroleum production. I've also consulted the governors of Texas, Alaska and other oil-producing states in order to educate myself on this issue."

The people again began to talk among themselves. Jillian waited for the buzz to subside, but it didn't. Once again, Moore asked the audience to give her the floor.

Jillian pulled in a deep breath. "We need to be sure that anything we do to help our economy won't endanger the fragile ecosystem in the gulf. Not only—"

A man at the back of the room shouted, "So, Governor, you want to ruin our fishing and kill our tourism?"

Jillian scanned the faces, but couldn't pick out the heckler. She saw Dave take several steps in the direction of the voice.

"On the contrary," she said firmly into the microphone. "I want to make sure we don't do that. I have solid plans for developing renewable energy sources while we investigate this further. We want to be sure a project this big is truly good for Maine before we put a lot of money into it."

"You sound like a bureaucrat, lady! You've sold out to Washington."

Jillian's heart raced and she felt her face flush. She clenched her teeth and zeroed in on the man who had shouted. Dave and two other security officers moved toward him through the crowd.

As the officers took hold of the man's arms and turned him toward the door, she forced herself to smile. "Thank you for your input."

The people in the nearer rows chuckled.

"Maybe now would be a good time to make your exit," Louis Moore said quietly.

She smiled at the audience. "Again, thank you for coming."

Stephanie was at Jillian's elbow. A few steps away, Andrew was clearing a path for them toward the nearest door. The moderator tapped on the lectern with his gavel. "Folks, calm down or we'll have to dismiss the hearing."

In her peripheral vision, Jillian caught a glimpse of Dave and the officers hustling the heckler down the hallway toward the exit. Andrew walked quickly ahead of her toward the elevator. Stephanie stayed a step behind her all the way.

As they left the elevator and crossed the open area toward Jillian's office, the guard swung the door open. She and the two detectives went inside, and he closed it behind them.

Jillian looked at Andrew and Stephanie. "Whew."

Lettie rose and hurried toward her. "What happened? Bad crowd?"

"It got a little dicey," Andrew admitted. "Governor, maybe you should sit down."

"Yes," Lettie said. "Can I get you some tea?"

"Thank you, that sounds good." Jillian walked to her inner office and sank into the chair behind her desk. A public meeting had never shaken her so much. Was it just that one man, or did the whole roomful of people oppose her? Or were these jitters because of the shootings?

Lettie entered a few minutes later with a cup of tea on a tray, followed by Stephanie.

"Are you all right?" Lettie asked.

Jillian nodded and reached for the china cup. "Yes. I shouldn't have been surprised. I got a little taste of this during the campaign. But today . . ."

Stephanie nodded. "That guy was a little scary."

"They'd all been through a metal detector, though," Lettie added.

"Yes." Stephanie's voice held some reservation, and Jillian looked up at her quickly.

"Do you think the environmentalists planted that heckler?" she asked.

"I don't know. Our investigators will look into it, you can be sure." Stephanie grinned. "Dave Hutchins and Carl Millbridge are probably duking it out right now over who gets to question that guy."

TWELVE

Dave arrived at the Blaine House after dinner on Friday evening, almost three hours later than usual. Bob Caruthers met him on the stairs and directed him to the den next to Jillian's office. Dave stopped in the doorway, surveying Jillian curled up in a recliner. Naomi sat on the sofa with a large bowl of popcorn on her lap. Both were watching television.

"Oh, hello, Dave." Jillian lowered the footrest of her chair.

"Hello, ladies. Please don't get up. It wasn't my intention to interrupt you when you're getting a little relaxation for a change."

Jillian shook her head and stood. "I know you're late because you're putting in overtime on my case."

Naomi kept her place on the couch, but smiled a greeting. Jillian led him to the connecting door and into her office. Dave noted that it was the first time he'd seen her in casual attire—black pants and a soft, powder-blue pullover. She looked great. But Dave thought she looked great no matter what she was wearing. He hoped today's events hadn't upset her too badly.

They sat down and Jillian gave him a weak

smile. "I'm told you've questioned the man who made such a ruckus at the hearing this afternoon."

"Yes. We let him cool his heels for a few hours while we did a detailed background check, and then let him go."

"Who is he?"

Dave pulled out his pocket notebook. "Nathan Sedge. He's worked on the Green Party campaign for the last three elections. He's against oil drilling, wind turbines, river dams for electrical power stations—you name it, he hates it. And nuclear power plants are anathema to this guy."

"Okay. How does he expect us to heat our homes and get to work? I'm sure he didn't walk to the hearing this afternoon."

"I think he wants someone else to bring oil and coal to the Maine-New Hampshire border and sell it to us there without stepping foot over the line. He envisions a pristine Maine in our future."

Jillian put a hand to her forehead and sighed. "Would you join me for coffee?"

"Absolutely."

She picked up the phone and spoke into it quietly. As she hung up, her brow creased in thought. "Do you think this man is harmless?"

"I think he intended to call attention to his cause today. In fact, he may even have gone to the hearing intending to get arrested."

Jillian gazed at him. "Stephanie thought he

might have been planted by the anti-oil lobbyists."

"Sure. Anything's possible. But you're not really opposed to his cause. He tried to paint you as an out-and-out industrialist, but you're not. My opinion is, he just wanted to stir up some media coverage."

Coffee and dessert arrived. As Beth set out plates of cheesecake, Jillian rose and moved to a chair near the small table.

"I wonder if Naomi would like to join us."

"I believe she's retired, ma'am," Beth said.

Jillian looked at the clock. "It's later than I thought. After nine already."

Beth left the room a moment later, and Dave studied Jillian as she poured their coffee.

"Are you tired?" he asked. "Don't let me keep you up."

"No. I'd like to discuss this a bit more."

Her smile still enchanted him. If anything, weathering the trials of the past two months had enhanced her beauty. He imagined what it would be like to tell her so.

"I've asked my mother if she'd like to come live with me here," Jillian said.

Dave accepted a mug and cradled it between his hands. "That's great. You could spend more time together."

Jillian shook her head. "She said no. She doesn't want to leave her house empty."

"I'm sorry."

She turned mournful eyes on him. "She also says she doesn't feel safe here."

Dave looked down, groping for a comforting reply.

"In fact," Jillian went on, "she's pestering me to move home again. She thinks I have a better chance of living out my term if I don't stay here."

Dave set his coffee on a coaster. "Is that what you think?"

Jillian shook her head, clamping her mouth in a thin line. "No. It would just cause a lot of headaches for you and the rest of the EPU."

"You're right. It would be harder to protect you at your house in Belgrade, and the traveling back and forth would present greater risks."

Her large, blue eyes held his gaze, and he wanted desperately to ease her mind.

"We'll find out who was behind the shootings. Maybe then Mrs. Clark will come and stay with you for a while, if not permanently."

She exhaled slowly. After a sip of her coffee, she glanced up at him and smiled. "Our chef makes fantastic cheesecake. You've got to try it."

He eyed the plate nearest him. "That looks positively decadent. Will you join me?"

"Why not? It's been a stressful day."

Dave nodded. "Comfort food. Dig in, Governor."

Her eyes flickered, but she reached for her dessert. She took a bite, closed her eyes, chewed and smiled. "Perfect. Let's talk about something else."

"Not cheesecake?"

She laughed, and the sound set a flood of warmth through him. "I meant, not the shootings or today's hearing or Mom. What are you doing this weekend?"

"Uh . . . I plan to go ice fishing with some buddies of mine."

"Hmm. That surprises me."

"Why?"

She shrugged and smiled at him mysteriously as she cut another piece of the cheesecake with her fork.

He popped a bite into his mouth. After a moment, he realized she wasn't going to answer. Should he let her off the hook? He couldn't resist—he had to know. "Why does it surprise you?" he asked again.

"I don't know. I guess I figured you for skiing or taking a date to the ice show in Portland."

"I've got a couple of friends who like to go ice fishing. One of them is handicapped. Getting out on a lake with his fishing gear makes him feel like he's on a level playing field with the rest of us." He took another bite.

"Isn't it late in the season?"

"It's been cold this winter. The ice is still good."

Jillian set her plate aside and reached for her mug. "How long have you known this friend?"

"About five years."

"Since Iraq?"

"You're good."

"Just call me Sherlock." She smiled, then sobered. "He was injured there?"

Dave nodded. "He was in my unit. The only kid who got hurt." He grimaced at the memory. "I thought we were heading home scot-free, but two weeks before our tour was up, a roadside bomb got him. He lost a leg at the knee."

"How great that you kept in touch, and that you still do things with him."

Dave looked down at the half piece of cheesecake on his plate. Why should he be here now, eating dessert with a beautiful woman? It wasn't chance that had brought him home safe, twice, when so many hadn't made it. God had engineered every day of his life. But he still felt unworthy.

"I try to keep up with the men who served under me."

"You were an officer."

"Sergeant."

She nodded gravely. "And now you're serving here."

He smiled slightly. "I like my job."

"I guess this is a piece of cake compared to Iraq."

"Yeah. Cherry cheesecake."

They both laughed. He looked intently at her

face, and she didn't look away.

"What are you doing this weekend?" he asked finally.

"I'm going to my mom's tomorrow. And I'll probably go visit a couple of my law partners. On Sunday morning, I'll go to church here in Augusta, then meet with a group of Swedish businessmen."

"You have to work Sunday?"

She raised her shoulders in a helpless shrug. "I'm governor 24/7, and that afternoon is the only time our schedules would allow. I'm entertaining them in the reception room downstairs to discuss exporting some Maine products to Sweden."

He wondered if so many plans in so many places on the weekend was a good idea, even with Stevenson gone. On the other hand, getting out of her routine and her usual territory—even with a couple of EPU officers in tow—might be good for Jillian.

"If you weren't busy, I'd invite you to go fishing with us."

"Ha. Sure you would." Her laugh warmed him again—better than the coffee did.

Dave was surprised when Bob Caruthers tapped on the door.

"Yes, Bob?" Jillian smiled, remaining relaxed in her chair.

"I just wanted to let you know I'm leaving,

ma'am. Ryan and Penny will be with you overnight."

Dave looked at his watch, amazed at how much time had passed.

"Thank you," Jillian said, and Bob closed the door.

Dave stood and stretched his arms. "I didn't realize it was so late. Sorry I kept you up so long."

Jillian's pert smile set his stomach tumbling. "Hey, I'm not the one who has to get up at the crack of dawn and go sit in a freezing little shack on the ice."

"For your information, ma'am, we'll have a heater and plenty of coffee and sandwiches."

"Ah." She stood, grinning. "I wish I could go."

"No, you don't."

"Sure I do. I like to fish. And the idea of being out on Messalonskee or Great Pond sounds very attractive right now."

He gave her a sage wink. "I don't think your entourage would fit in the shack with us. Maybe in another four years I'll ask you to go ice fishing." He headed for the door, struggling to get his goofy smile under control before he came face-to-face with Ryan or Penny.

"If you do, I'll say yes."

Dave stopped in his tracks. He turned slowly, his pulse rocketing. Jillian's face was stone-cold sober as she watched him. The look in her eyes drew him irresistibly. He took two steps toward

155

her before he could stop himself. They stood a yard apart, eyeing each other. Jillian's eyes flickered and she pulled in a quick breath.

He knew what he wanted to do, but duty wrapped itself around him stronger than the longing in her blue eyes.

"Jillian—"

"I know." She raised one hand, but whether she meant to reach for him or signal him to hold his ground, he wasn't sure. A soft tap on the door caused them both to step a few more inches apart.

"Come in," Jillian called.

Penny opened the door, took one look at the two of them, and lowered her gaze to the rug. "I'm sorry, Governor. I didn't know you had company. When I passed Miss Plante's room on my rounds, she asked if I knew where you were."

"I'm just about to retire," Jillian said. "Please tell her I'll be along in a minute."

"Yes, ma'am."

Penny disappeared, but left the door open.

"Good night, Dave."

Jillian held out her hand again, but this time there was no question of her purpose. He shook it, ignoring his desire to pull her into his arms.

"Good night, Governor. Thanks again for the coffee."

He left without looking back. Ryan stood outside the office door. Bob must have told him where the governor was before he left and put Ryan on duty here. Why hadn't Ryan told Penny that Dave was with the governor? Better yet, he could have simply told her the governor was still in her office and to mind her own business.

He raised his eyebrows at Ryan, barely pausing in the hall. Ryan shrugged, throwing him a silent it's-not-my-fault plea before he looked miserably toward the open doorway.

It wasn't worth hashing it over with Ryan, especially not now, with Jillian still in the room behind him. Dave hurried down the stairs. As he pulled on his coat near the security office, Penny came in from the game room.

"Awfully late for a briefing," she said with a frown.

"Couldn't help it."

"Well, it looked as though you were both enjoying it."

Dave stared at her. The idea that Penny was jealous shocked him. First off, he'd never given Penny any signals. Second, the idea of the elegant Jillian Goff falling for a working man like him was ludicrous.

Or was it? He pressed his lips firmly together as he zipped his jacket. The charged air in the office upstairs had nearly crackled between him and Jillian for a moment tonight.

No, he told himself. That was silly. He was just another member of her staff, like all the other EPU officers. They were almost part of the furniture.

"Good night, Penny." He went out the side door and headed for his pickup, shaking his head. Even if he were so stupid as to try to initiate something with the person he was protecting—against EPU regulations, of course—Jillian Goff was far too smart to do something like that. She was determined to fulfill her office without making any foolish mistakes. Falling for one of her security team was the type of slipup a woman of her caliber just didn't make.

THIRTEEN

You're off this case, Hutchins."

"But, sir—"

"Off the case. What don't you understand?"

Dave clamped his jaw shut.

Colonel Smith paced from his desk to the file cabinets at one side of the room and back. "And if you can't behave professionally, you'll be removed from the unit and demoted."

Dave's head swam. He couldn't lose his job for eating cheesecake with Jillian at her request. Could he?

"Sir, there was no unprofessional conduct by either me or the governor Friday night."

"Your colleagues say otherwise."

"My colleagues?" Dave swallowed hard.

"Yes. I've spoken to several EPU officers assigned to the Blaine House. Apparently, this wasn't your first cozy chat with the governor."

Penny. She must have gone to Smith, and Smith had called in the others and grilled them. Ryan, for sure. Probably Bob and Stephanie, too. Maybe Andrew.

"Sir, if I may explain—"

"No explanation needed, Hutchins. She's a beautiful woman. But a person hired to protect a public figure has a responsibility to keep the relationship professional."

There was that word again. Dave stared straight ahead while the colonel continued.

"Members of this unit are the elite of the state police. It's a highly coveted assignment, as you know. But the rules are clear. If a member of the Executive Protection Unit develops a personal relationship with a person he is responsible for protecting, it compromises his judgment. That officer cannot keep his position." The colonel turned and glared at him.

"Sir, if I may—"

"You may not. Your duties for the next month are confined to state police headquarters. Lieutenant Wilson will give you your daily assignments. You will do whatever investigative research you can from within those walls."

"Sir, that will curtail my usefulness to the—"

"If the other detectives have leads that you can follow discreetly, fine. But you are to have no personal contact with the governor. No phone calls, no e-mails."

"Sir, I would never phone or e-mail the governor."

"Good. I will review your situation at the end of one month."

When he stopped talking, the silence hung heavy between them.

"Yes, sir," Dave managed at last.

• • •

Thursday night Jillian entertained her old law partner, Margaret Harris, and her husband, Eric, with an informal dinner. Naomi had decided to go out with Beth's cousin again, so only three sat down in the family dining room.

"This is all so elegant, Jillian." Margaret surveyed the room with approval. "The food is wonderful, and I can't see anything wrong with the service, either."

"The staff is top-notch," Jillian said. "I don't have to lift a finger. Sometimes I wonder if I'm not getting lazy."

"Lazy?" Eric laughed. "You're working yourself to death."

"I hope you're not still stressed about everything that's happened." Margaret eyed her carefully. "You look wonderful, but if you need a break . . ."

"Yes, come and stay a few days with us anytime, Jillian. Get away from all this." Eric lifted his delicate blue-and-white china cup bearing the state seal, part of the service designed especially for the governor's residence, and sipped his coffee.

Margaret leaned toward her and lowered her voice. "You're safe now, right?"

Jillian forced a smile. "The state police still hope to find a motive for the shootings." She tried not to let distress show on her face.

Instead of Dave, Detective Carl Millbridge had come to the Blaine House to update her this week. Millbridge was about as cheerful and optimistic as a moose in the middle of the freeway. When she'd inquired about Dave, he had simply said Hutchins had been assigned elsewhere and would not be briefing her in the future. The session took all of five minutes. No coffee, no friendly conversation, no encouragement. No Dave.

"I think this whole thing about there being a conspiracy is crazy," Margaret said. "The guy was nuts and now he's dead."

Eric shook his head. "You never know. He could have been a hit man. Best to let the cops do a thorough job of investigating."

"Well, I certainly hope they find out for sure soon," Margaret said. "What's on your schedule for the next few weeks?"

A safer topic. Jillian gestured to Beth, who stood in the pantry doorway, and she silently removed their plates.

"I expect I'll be closeted in my office at the Capitol all of next week with various committee members. We're trying to cover a lot of ground with this session of the legislature. But I believe I'll be let out for the opening of the Elder Exposition at the Civic Center on Thursday."

Beth entered with a tray of pastries and fresh coffee. Jillian eyed the lemon tarts and éclairs.

"Please set that as far from me as possible after you serve my guests, Beth."

"Yes, ma'am." With a ghost of a smile, Beth offered the tray to Margaret and Eric, and then set it at the far end of the table within Eric's reach.

"And there's a memorial service Sunday afternoon for the trooper who was killed in the line of duty last week."

"Tragic thing," Margaret said.

"Yes. A terrible loss." Jillian crumpled her napkin and exhaled. That would be one of her most challenging public appearances. She had labored hard over the words she would speak to the dead trooper's family. She sent up a silent prayer for God's peace and guidance.

She was all nerves today, feeling out of sorts. And she knew exactly why. She had come to look forward to her meetings with Dave, because he grounded her, he kept her calm. The thought of no longer seeing him regularly—or at all—was almost more than she could stand. She needed to see him and find out what had happened.

Dave saw Jillian across the large auditorium. She inched toward the front of the church, surrounded by clergymen and EPU officers. For a second a pain slashed through him. He should be one of those closest to her, ensuring her safety, ready to comfort her if the tragic situation overwhelmed her.

He shook himself—it was exactly that kind of thinking that got him in trouble. He took his place to one side of the door. Another trooper, also in full dress uniform, stood gravely on the other side. Several more officers formed an honor guard on the steps of the church outside.

He sent up a swift prayer for the slain officer's family, and another for Jillian. *Lord, she's in Your hands. Please keep her safe. And help me not to think of myself as more important than I am. She doesn't need me, and that's a good thing. Thank You, though, for letting me get to know her.*

At that moment, before taking her seat beside the deceased's widow, Jillian turned and scanned the auditorium. Her eyes rested on Dave just for an instant. Then she looked away and began talking to someone.

Did she even know why he'd kept aloof all week? Why he'd stopped coming to the Blaine House? What had Carl told her about him when he'd gone to update her? Or had she even asked? Yes, she had. She must have. She would want to know.

He was determined to stop thinking about her for the next hour, and at all costs to avoid staring at her. Enough trouble had come his way. His career was at stake, not to mention Jillian's reputation. He mustn't give any indication that he cared about her in a personal way.

Sheer grit got him through the memorial service. Afterward, the church emptied, and the honor guard was dismissed to follow the hearse to the crypt. As he walked with several other officers toward the waiting car, Andrew ran across the snowy parking lot to catch him.

"Dave, wait up!"

Andrew wore plain clothes today, fulfilling his role with Stephanie as one of Jillian's closest guards. His face was red from his exertion and the cold.

"What's up?" Dave asked, stopping a few feet from the car and letting the other men go ahead without him.

"The governor." Andrew cast a quick look over his shoulder. "She wants you to have tea with her and Miss Plante tomorrow."

Dave looked past him. Jillian was already in the Lincoln. Stephanie slid into the backseat and closed the door.

"I can't, Andrew."

"Busy?"

Dave frowned at him. "Don't you know? The colonel reassigned me. I can't talk to the governor."

Andrew's puzzled look told him that word hadn't gotten around the unit as quickly as he'd assumed it would.

"I'm not allowed to speak to her," Dave repeated.

Andrew's eyes grew round. "For real?"

Dave nodded. "Just tell her that I'm sorry, but I've been reassigned. Against my wishes," he added. Looking closely at Andrew to make sure he understood, taking a risk.

Andrew nodded and extended his hand.

"Sorry, man," he said. "I'm sure whatever this is will blow over."

"Thanks. Let's hope so."

Lieutenant Wilson flagged Dave down after the EPU's daily briefing two weeks later.

"Hutchins, I need you to fill in for Ryan Mills this afternoon."

Dave smiled. "Sure." Any change would be good. He was already sick of shuffling reports in the office and would be glad to get out into the fresh air.

Wilson hesitated and glanced toward the door. "Look, we both know what you're in the doghouse for. But I'm desperate here."

Dave stopped breathing for a moment.

"It's just for this afternoon—I'll assign someone else to take over Mills's duties for the rest of the week. Somehow, his vacation schedule slipped by me. But if you can be at the governor's office at quarter to five and help escort her home for the night, it will get me off the hook."

"Sure."

Wilson looked at Dave closely, frowned and rubbed his left eyebrow. "Maybe this isn't such a good idea."

"I assure you, I'll stick to regulations, sir," Dave said quickly.

Wilson gritted his teeth. "The colonel expressly said that he doesn't want you on Blaine House duty."

"With all due respect, sir, the only thing I'm guilty of is having a piece of cheesecake at the governor's request during a briefing. That's it."

Wilson sighed and lowered the clipboard. "Okay, but keep this low-profile. Just stay with her until the night shift arrives, and then get out of there. And keep your distance. You drive. There'll be another officer with you." He squinted down at the list in his hand. "Caruthers. Once you get her home, let Caruthers stick close to the governor. You can make the rounds of the perimeter."

"Thanks for trusting me, Lieutenant."

Wilson sighed and shook his head. "I'll probably take some flak if the colonel finds out, but it would take me an hour to switch everyone's schedule around. That's if I could find someone off duty who would come in. I'm counting on you, Hutchins."

"I understand, sir." Dave headed back to his desk, restraining himself from pumping a victorious fist in the air.

Vera Clark had come to spend a couple of nights in the mansion with her daughter. At dinner that evening, Vera and Naomi kept up a steady stream of chatter. Jillian forced herself not to look toward the doorway every few seconds. She firmly declined dessert, even though Amelia, the chef, had made her signature apple pie. She sipped black coffee as Beth served her mother and Naomi their dessert.

Dave's appearance at the statehouse early that evening had surprised her. Lettie had come into her office and closed the door.

"Detectives Caruthers and Hutchins are here to escort you home whenever you're ready."

"Dave?" she'd said, sounding like an excited high school girl.

"That's correct." Lettie smiled and exited as quietly as she'd come.

Jillian was glad she'd had warning. It gave her a few minutes to school her features and get her pulse under control before she announced that she was ready to leave for the night. While Bob Caruthers seemed like a diligent civil servant, she couldn't be sure he wasn't the one who had made trouble for Dave. She'd ruled out Stephanie. Andrew had seemed stunned by Dave's suspension. That left Bob, Penny and Ryan as candidates for "most likely to rat on your colleague."

Unless one of the Blaine House staff had said

something. Beth? The chef? One of the maids? Jillian was on good terms with all of them and couldn't imagine any of them lodging a complaint. Especially when the "crime" was so innocuous. A cup of coffee and cheesecake with an EPU officer. Not even one on protection duty.

Okay, several cups of coffee, and a couple of heart-to-heart talks. She knew the protocol. Elected officials were not to advance personal relationships with those who served them. She had crossed a very thin line and embarked on a wonderful friendship with Dave, which had now been torn away from them. She missed him terribly. Knowing he was somewhere in the building made it extremely hard to concentrate on what her mother was saying.

"That will be charming, Naomi." Her mother looked at Jillian. "Are you all right, dear? You look a little pale."

"I'm fine." Jillian placed her cup carefully on the blue-and-white saucer.

"You're working too hard."

"No, I'm absolutely fine." She smiled across at Naomi. "Where did you say you were taking Mom tomorrow?"

"She'd like to visit the new specialty stores at the Marketplace."

"You'll like that, Mom," Jillian said. She was glad Naomi could spare the time to entertain her mother while business claimed her own attention. Tomorrow, Andrew would drive her to Lewiston to see a new urban-renewal project.

When they had finished dessert, the three women moved upstairs to the family living room.

"What about this big charity event coming up, Jillian?" Vera asked.

"That's not until June, but plans are taking shape. There'll be a big fund-raiser to bring in money to expand the state library. All of the living former governors have been invited, and I'll entertain them and their wives here, in the state dining room, along with our congressional delegation."

"That's very exciting." Her mother smiled. "I'd love to be here. What are you going to wear?"

"I haven't even thought about it," Jillian confessed.

"You need a new gown," Naomi said.

"Well, I've still got the one I didn't wear for the inaugural ball."

"No, no, no," her mother cried. "Darling, that was for a January event, and this will be in June. That dress won't be at all suitable."

"I suppose you're right, but I've got three months to think about it. Are you going out with Beth's cousin again, Naomi?" Jillian asked, in an effort to change the subject. "What's his name?"

Naomi shrugged. "Sean. I don't know. He's really not my type." She looked toward the doorway and lowered her voice. "I'll tell you something, though."

"What?" Vera asked.

"When I went down to Brunswick last week to see Sean, he took me to Portland. We went to a club, and we ran into a friend of his, Jack Kendall. And guess what?"

Jillian eyed her for a moment and suddenly she knew. "You liked the friend better than you liked Sean."

"Isn't that terrible?" Naomi looked eagerly to her and Vera, obviously wanting them to deny it.

"This Sean has no claim on you, does he?" Vera asked.

"No, but it felt a little awkward."

Low voices in the hallway drew Jillian's gaze to the open doorway. She was almost certain that Dave was nearby. Would they ever be able to have a normal conversation again? They'd barely spoken a word on the short ride between the statehouse and the mansion. With Dave driving and Bob beside her in the backseat, a strained silence had settled in.

So why had Dave showed up tonight? He wasn't part of the team that usually protected her, and she'd thought he was confined to quarters, so to speak. Andrew had said in so many words that Dave was forbidden to see her. Colonel

171

Smith probably gave the order, in an effort to avoid what he imagined was a brewing scandal.

She wished she could catch Dave when no one else was around and find out what was really going on. But someone always hovered nearby. Could she buttonhole another of the EPU officers—Stephanie perhaps?

She sank back in her chair with a sigh. Better to leave it alone. The less people talked about her nonrelationship with Dave, the sooner the speculation would die down. Not that she believed there really was much speculation outside the Executive Protection Unit. There was nothing to it—nothing at all. So why did she feel guilty?

FOURTEEN

Vera and Naomi dressed fashionably but warmly for their shopping expedition the next morning. Jillian almost wished she could escape with them.

They had just left the breakfast table when Andrew announced that Colonel Smith had arrived and wished to speak with her in private. Though his expression remained neutral, Andrew's eyes darted about, refusing to focus on her face. Jillian felt a bit light-headed as she instructed him to show the colonel to her private office upstairs. She assured her mother it was probably a minor detail involving security for her Lewiston trip, and practically shoved her and Naomi out the door.

Before mounting the staircase, she sent up a quick prayer. Smith's only other visitations to her at the Blaine House had occurred on the mornings following shooting incidents. What now? She squared her shoulders and marched to her office.

Smith's cheeks were infused with a deep red, and his brow furrowed as he turned to face her.

"I hate to be the bearer of bad news, ma'am, but one of the early morning radio talk show hosts called me and asked if you have a . . . uh . . . love interest."

"Oh?" Jillian felt the blood shoot to her face. She reached her chair and sat down quickly. "I hope you said no."

Smith cleared his throat. "Well, I didn't think I had the authority to say one way or the other, ma'am."

She pulled in a long, slow breath and held it for a moment. "Did he name names?"

"No, ma'am."

She shot off a silent *Thank You, Lord*. "Good, because the whole thing is preposterous. What do you recommend as a course of action?"

"I've called Mark Payson. He'll be here in a few minutes to discuss it."

Jillian glanced at her wristwatch. "I'm sorry. I'm expected at the statehouse soon. I have a meeting at nine."

"This is more important."

How could he possibly know what her meeting was about? On second thought, he probably knew exactly whom she was scheduled to meet with all morning. She recalled something about Lettie faxing a copy of her schedule to the colonel and Lieutenant Wilson every evening.

"Do you think so? It's only gossip."

"Gossip can cause you more problems than you imagine."

"All right. Did he say where he got his so-called information?"

" 'A source close to the governor.' That's all he'd say. Of course I threatened to take it to his boss if they said one word on the air."

Jillian's stomach fluttered worse than it had on inauguration day. "It's ridiculous."

"Is it?" He stared hard at her.

"Yes, of course."

The colonel pulled a ringing cell phone out of his pocket. As he opened it, he turned away from her, toward the window. "Yes?"

Her heart pounded as she waited. Had her enemies found a way to ruin her without killing her? Starting a scandal was much less risky than committing murder.

After a moment, the colonel put the phone away. "Payson's on his way up."

The public information officer entered the room half a minute later, carrying a computer disk.

"Governor. Colonel. I'm trying to put this fire out before it starts, but a television reporter handed me this as I left my office." Payson looked toward Jillian's desk. "Does your computer have a DVD player?"

"Yes." Jillian followed him to the desk and watched him insert the disk.

"The television station intends to run some footage of you on their evening report tonight."

Jillian and the colonel stood by him to watch

the video. The screen showed the SUV Jillian used pulling into the private driveway behind the Blaine House. When the vehicle stopped, Bob Caruthers got out and held the door for her as she exited and headed for the family entrance of the mansion.

She gasped. "Where were they? Did they come onto the grounds?"

"Long lens," Smith muttered. "Probably across the street, near the exit to the parking garage. When was this taken? Can you tell?"

"Well . . ." She rubbed her forehead and thought. "Bob was one of my escorts last evening. He or Andrew Browne usually brings me over from the office. Or Ryan Mills." She didn't dare mention that Dave had been driving last night. Did the colonel know?

"The woman who gave me this asked if it was true you had a romantic liaison with one of your bodyguards," Payson said.

Jillian flushed. "So . . . they think I'm in love with Bob Caruthers?"

"She didn't say so."

The colonel shook his head. "Someone called them with a tip, the same as the radio talk show. Caruthers just happened to be on hand when they came and shot film."

Jillian wheeled away and walked to the window. "That's all rubbish. Someone's trying to make trouble for me."

The colonel replayed the video. "Footage of the governor getting out of her car, with an EPU officer escorting her. No physical contact. No anything. Just general footage, that's all."

Payson sighed and straightened. "I advised them not to run it, and I said I'd call the reporter after I viewed it. I hope we can trace this thing back and find out where the rumor started."

Jillian held out a hand in supplication. "There's nothing to it. You both know that, don't you?"

"I have no reason to think otherwise," said Payson.

"Mr. Payson, I'd like you to work with my PR team on this. Please get them up to speed." She was determined to hold his gaze, no matter what gymnastics her stomach performed.

"I will. Then we'll make a joint statement."

"So the governor can carry on with her planned agenda for today?" Colonel Smith asked.

"Yes. The best way to quash this rumor is to give the media nothing that substantiates it." Payson turned to Jillian. "The EPU needs to be careful not to give wrong impressions. The colonel can speak to them. Have you gotten friendly with some of the officers?"

Jillian gulped. "I suppose so. I mean, they're with me day and night. We chat a little."

Payson nodded. "We have another female detective approaching eligibility for this unit. I think the more female officers assigned to you the better right now." He looked at Smith. "Let's try to have at least one woman on duty here every night."

"Governor, do you have any idea how this rumor started?" Smith asked, frowning.

"I—No." Jillian went back to her desk and sat down. "I've met with one of the EPU detectives for a briefing twice a week since I took office, but that officer isn't one of those assigned here at the Blaine House. There have been times when I've invited officers to share a cup of coffee with me or sit down for a few minutes and talk."

"Do they?" Payson asked.

"If they're going off duty, they might stay and chat a few minutes, but when they're on duty, they politely refuse. It's a rather lonely existence here, Mr. Payson."

He eyed her for a long moment, then dropped his gaze. "I'm sorry. These officers are required to keep a professional demeanor. But that doesn't mean they can't be friendly, especially when no visitors are present."

"I should hope not. I need to know them and trust them."

"Yes." Payson sighed and looked at the colonel. "I think that's all. Speak to the officers and remind them that someone is always watching."

Without fanfare, about a week later, Wilson put Dave back in the field. A pleasant warmth filled

Dave as he stared at the assignment board. After the briefing he ducked into the lieutenant's office.

"There's no mystery about it," Wilson told him. "We need you back out there on the job. You're one of our best investigators, and the colonel knows it."

"Thanks." Dave hesitated. "You . . . uh . . . put me down to drive the governor to Portland on Thursday."

"That's right. There will be a female officer along, too." Wilson tipped his chair back and looked up at the ceiling. "In the old days, the governor would jump in the car with a driver, and off he'd go. We can't do that anymore. Governor Goff needs at least two security officers all the time. And it's starting to look like one of those two should be a woman, just to keep the gossip down. Smith's little internal investigation didn't turn up anything solid against you, so I figure that I can put you on driving detail now and then. Just don't sit around and chitchat with the governor, eh?"

Dave nodded. "You got it."

The hour-long drive to Portland flew for Jillian. She spent most of it going over the briefings Lettie had prepared for her appointments in the city—one with Portland's mayor and his staff, and another with the administrators of the University of Southern Maine. She also chatted with

179

Penny, who was next to her, for a few minutes.

Penny was not her favorite of the security officers. In repose, Penny seemed to wear a habitual frown. Jillian received the distinct impression that Penny disapproved of her, though she had no clue why.

During the ride, Penny leaned forward four times to ask Dave a question. Jillian had greeted him in what she hoped was a discreet fashion and deliberately hadn't attempted further conversation with him. Penny, however, seemed determined to get his attention.

So maybe that was it, Jillian reflected. Dave seemed to get along well with all the officers who guarded her, treating them equally. Perhaps that wasn't enough for Penny.

The meeting with the university administrators went well, and afterward Jillian spoke briefly to a gathering of student leaders. Dave then drove them to city hall, where she joined the mayor in his office. Penny sat just behind her at the table, while Dave stood near the door. Jillian was glad the seating placed her with her back to him. She wouldn't be tempted to look at him.

Shortly after her arrival, the door opened and the city treasurer and several city council members walked in, including chairman Peter Harrison. Jillian stood, her chest tightening. It was her first encounter with the man who lost the election to her in November.

"Peter. How have you been?" She extended her hand, and he took it with a tight smile.

"I've been fine. I've followed your progress on the news—seems you've had a few rough moments."

She assumed he was referring to the shootings. All through their meeting, while the mayor went on about the city's symbiosis with the state government, Harrison sat stiffly, avoiding her gaze. He offered little to the discussion, though Jillian once made a point of asking him a question to draw him in. At last the meeting ended, cordially on all counts. She walked out to the parking lot with Dave ahead and Penny at her side.

When they were safely in the vehicle, Dave put the SUV in gear and headed for the highway. Jillian couldn't ride all the way back to Augusta without releasing some steam—she'd explode.

"Dave?"

"Yes?" He met her gaze in the rearview mirror.

"Could we get something to eat? Penny and I had coffee, but I'm starved, and you must be, too."

He grinned at her. "Fine by me, but no restaurants. We've only got the two of us for security."

"Drive-up burgers are fine. I can even duck down and hide while you order."

He laughed. "I think the tinted glass will take care of that. Penny?"

"Sounds good to me," Penny said.

Once they had their orders, Dave pulled into a large grocery store's parking area. He drove to a spot far from the store, where few people had left their vehicles.

Penny had already opened her container of salad, but Jillian waited until Dave shut the engine off.

"Would you mind asking the blessing, Dave?"

Penny's eyes flared for a moment, but she said nothing.

"Sure. If you don't mind me keeping my eyes open."

Jillian chuckled. "Whatever you need to do."

After a moment's silence, Dave's voice came, low and clear. "Dear Lord, thank You for safety today and productive meetings for the governor. We thank You for this food and for all Your blessings to us. Amen."

Jillian couldn't help smiling as she opened her salad and flatware pack. Penny waited until Jillian took a bite of her salad and then began to eat.

"Dave?" Jillian said.

He swung around and met her gaze directly. "Yes, ma'am?"

Jillian's heart lurched. Was the "ma'am" for Penny's benefit, or to remind her of the distance between them?

"I've been thinking about Peter Harrison." She

looked over at Penny, to include her in the conversation. "Do either of you think he's still bitter about losing the election?"

"He certainly seemed on edge today," Penny said, "but I don't know if that was from being in the same room with you or not."

Dave frowned slightly. "Do you think he might be bitter enough to hire someone to kill you?"

Jillian shivered as she exhaled. She hadn't wanted to meet that thought head-on, but it lurked there in the back of her mind. "It seems horribly unjust to think it of him."

They continued eating in silence. A few minutes later, Dave took their food containers to a trash can and then headed once more for Augusta. Jillian sank back on the seat and closed her eyes. Fatigue set in, and she tried to let go of the questions that nagged her. Even so, images kept popping into her mind. Peter Harrison, apparently still holding a grudge. Roderick Tanger, simmering in prison. Parker Tilton, perhaps overly ambitious. Raymond Grant, who would go to great lengths to see the Gulf of Maine on the Environmental Protection Agency's list of approved oil drilling sites. Gerald Francis, whom she had helped put away for several years on a manslaughter charge, and a recently released murderer she had helped prosecute. Was one of them biding his time, waiting for another chance to strike? If not, who else was out there watching her?

"So, Dave," Penny said quietly. Jillian felt the seat cushion compress as she leaned forward. "Are you going to Dick St. John's retirement party on Saturday?"

Dave said softly, "This really isn't the best time to discuss it."

The seat cushion shifted again as Penny sat back. Jillian sneaked a peek from beneath her lashes. Arms folded, frown in place. No, Penny was not happy.

Dusk settled around them and Jillian closed her eyes again. God was in control, and Dave was at the wheel. She let go of the troublesome questions and eased into pleasant oblivion.

FIFTEEN

Andrew met Dave at the bottom of the staircase leading up to the governor's family quarters on Friday evening.

"I got here as fast as I could," Dave said.

"She's in the den next to her office, waiting for you."

"Did you call Carl Millbridge?"

"The governor asked for you," he said.

Dave threw him a sideways glance. Andrew kept his expression neutral. They mounted the stairs, and Dave looked along the hallway. Beyond the entrance to the den, Stephanie stood on duty outside the office door. He nodded to her, turned in at the first doorway and swept his gaze over the room.

Naomi sat on the sofa with Jillian, one hand protectively on the governor's arm. Jillian's mouth was set in a tense line, but her eyes lit when she saw him and she straightened her shoulders. Beyond them, Penny stood before the connecting door into the office, and Bob bent over the windowsill, studying the woodwork.

Dave walked across the room, conscious that every eye followed him. He dropped into the chair nearest Jillian. She wore a cream-colored dress that draped her elegant figure to perfection. A necklace of light purple stones glittered at her throat.

"Are you all right?"

"Yes." She started to reach toward him, but pulled her hand back and clasped it tightly in the other on her lap, as though forcing herself not to touch him. "It seems like a small thing, but . . . I admit, I'm frightened."

He nodded. "Tell me exactly what happened."

"I came home late from the statehouse—about six o'clock. I was due for a dinner at the Calumet Club at seven, so Detective Millbridge wasn't coming tonight. One of the maids—Kelly—helped me change my clothes. We left about twenty minutes to seven." She cut her gaze to Andrew, who stood a yard away, and he nodded.

"Andrew drove you?" Dave asked.

"Yes. Bob went with us."

Dave looked up at Andrew. "Was anyone on duty here while you were gone?"

"Just Stephanie."

"Okay. So then what?" He looked back into Jillian's eyes.

"When we returned, I came upstairs and I stopped by Naomi's room. I hadn't seen her all day. We chatted for a few minutes. I was tired, but I wanted to look over my schedule before I undressed. I do that in the evening, so I don't have any surprises the next morning."

That was like her—always prepared. "So you went to your office?"

"Yes. The first thing I noticed was that several folders I'd left on the desk had been moved. I'd put the printout of Monday's schedule inside the top one, with notes Lettie had prepared for me about the first meeting of the day. But when I came in tonight, the schedule was on top of the folders."

"Oh? What's the meeting about?"

"A proposal for more wind turbines on the outer islands."

"Anything else?"

"I don't think so," Jillian said. "I looked in the file cabinets and in all my desk drawers. I think someone pawed around a little, but I can't say for certain that anything's missing. But my computer had been used."

"You're sure?"

She nodded. "The list of recent files opened includes a couple I haven't looked at for a while."

"And you didn't go into the office before you left for the dinner?"

Jillian shook her head.

"So it could have happened anytime between when you left this morning and when you got home after the dinner this evening?"

"No, I came over for lunch. That's when I dropped off the folders. About one o'clock, I'd say. Everything was fine then."

"I'd like to look around your office now." Dave went into the office and carefully examined Jillian's desk and the folders on it. Andrew watched him, not touching anything. Jillian peered in from the doorway.

"Let's take some prints off this desk," Dave said.

"Sure." Andrew turned toward Jillian. "Ma'am, whose prints can we expect to find on it?"

Jillian licked her lips, frowning. "Well, mine for sure. The staff—sometimes the maids come in to clean. Probably Naomi's. The administrative assistant down the hall. Maybe some of your EPU officers. How far back should we go? My mother's? And Colonel Smith was here a few weeks ago. The majority leader met with me in this room last week."

Dave sighed. The list was too long. But he could deal with it. He turned to Andrew.

"We need a list of everyone who's been in the house since the governor left her papers here at one o'clock."

Andrew took out his pocket notebook. "Stephanie and I have already started a list. We got the names of all the staffers who worked this afternoon—the chef and one kitchen helper, two maids, the administrative assistant and one clerk. Most of them left between 5:00 and 6:00 p.m. I also put down the security officer who was here during the day, Bob, me and Stephanie.

And then there was a tour group at two o'clock, with a total of ten people in the group. They toured the public rooms downstairs with the clerk I mentioned. I've been assured none of them left the tour area, but we've got the contact information if you want to talk to them."

"Okay, good." Dave looked at Jillian. Her shoulders shook. He walked toward her. "Why don't you sit down for a minute, ma'am?"

She sobbed then, and the tears let go. "I'm sorry."

"It's okay. Come on." He gently took her elbow and guided her to the big chair behind the desk.

Jillian sat down and pulled open a drawer, then drew her hand back. "Oh, you're going to take prints."

"Go ahead. It's fine."

She snatched a tissue from the drawer and put it to her eyelids.

Dave shot a glance toward the hall door. Penny stood, watching them.

"Penny, could you get the governor a cup of tea, please?" Dave called. "Hot and strong."

Penny nodded and disappeared. He looked around at the circle of faces. Bob, Naomi, Stephanie and Andrew had closed in a circle around the desk.

"Let's give the governor some space," Dave said.

"Sure." Andrew turned to the others. "Bob, take

the hall door. Stephanie, you stay with Miss Plante. I'll watch this entrance." He herded them out and quietly closed the door that connected to the den.

Dave ignored the chairs and went to his knees beside Jillian. She blotted her incredible blue eyes and focused on him.

"Thank you," she whispered raggedly. "I don't know why, but this shook me up more than anything else that's happened. Dave, someone was here, in my private space. How did this happen?"

"I don't know. The entrances are kept locked all day."

Her eyes widened. "The staff are all loyal. I mean . . . I think they are."

"One of the maids may have gotten curious and done a little snooping. Who knows? So, tell me—do you have a password on your computer?"

"To open it? No. I did." Jillian gritted her teeth. "It was such a pain, I took it off. Pretty stupid of me."

He reached for the mouse beside her keyboard. When the Microsoft Word program came up, he studied the list of opened files.

"I have an external hard drive for backup," Jillian said. "It saves every file I open."

"Great. We can find out when these files were accessed and see what else the snooper looked at." He faced her and laid one hand on the back of her chair. "I assure you, we'll take care of you. We'll increase the guard."

A tear rolled in slow motion down her cheek. It was more than he could bear. He stopped trying to resist and pulled her tenderly into his arms. She laid her head on his shoulder.

"Jillian, I'm so sorry this happened. I don't want you to be afraid."

She pulled in a deep, shuddering breath. "This is my nightmare. Not the intruder. Me taking it so hard. Dave, I can't fall apart. If it gets out that I cried . . ." She sobbed again, and he tightened his hold on her.

"It's okay. You're a strong person. Lately you've been under a lot of stress. Let it out now, and you'll be fine when you have to face people. I promise." He stroked her hair, wishing he could stay here forever and comfort her, but knowing he was pushing the envelope every second he held her. This was way more personal than the job warranted, and they both knew it.

Dave was about to walk out of his apartment Saturday morning when his phone rang.

"Hutchins? This is Lieutenant Wilson."

"Yes, sir?"

"I want to see you in my office. Now."

Dave didn't dare think about the reason for the summons. When he arrived at headquarters twenty minutes later, Colonel Smith and Wilson were both waiting for him. The meeting went quickly. Though Wilson seemed to choke on his words, Smith had no trouble pronouncing his sentence.

"This is it, Hutchins. You're taking a week off, and when you come back, you'll be assigned to the most boring drudge work we can dig up for you at the public safety office until further notice. No contact with the governor."

Dave could almost see smoke coming out his ears. "May I ask why, sir?"

"I'll tell you why. We received a tip this morning that you've been getting way too cozy with the governor, if you get my drift."

Dave clenched his fists and fought to control his outrage. "That's not true, sir."

"Whether it's true or not, I have to take it seriously. Can you give me a good reason not to?"

"Because it's a lie. Who delivered this so-called tip?"

The colonel looked him over and said carefully, "We have a policy. Employees need to be able to report violations without fearing that their privacy will be breached."

"It was a department employee, then."

"You're dismissed, Hutchins."

"But, sir, the investigation—"

Smith glared at him. "The rest of the team will have to get by without you."

"But—"

"I've talked to your colleagues. At least two of them say there's something between the two of you." Smith shook his head. "I wouldn't have thought she'd be that foolish."

"She's not. Sir, I assure you, nothing improper has happened or will happen between us. I'm sure the mere suggestion would be abhorrent to the governor."

Smith glared at him for a long moment, then turned his back. "My order stands. I never should have let Wilson put you back on the case."

Wilson winced and refused to meet Dave's gaze.

Smith headed for the door. "Any more of this nonsense, and you're back on traffic duty."

He exited, shutting the door forcefully behind him. After several seconds' silence, Wilson gritted his teeth and picked up a sheaf of papers from his desktop. "I'm sorry, Hutchins. He wanted to fire you, but I convinced him the allegations didn't merit that and that the evidence was thin anyway. I'm very sorry."

"Thanks for supporting me," Dave said. "But again, nothing happened."

"I believe you. But Colonel Smith hates being woken up on the weekend with bad news."

"What on earth are people saying? This is stupid."

Wilson nodded. "The implication was . . . sordid. Even if it's an outright lie, it's best if

193

you keep your distance from the governor. For her sake, as well as your own."

More than a week later, Andrew Browne arrived in the governor's Capitol office on Monday afternoon to escort her home. Jillian went to the doorway and caught his eye. Andrew walked toward her.

"All set, ma'am?"

"Actually, no." Jillian looked over his shoulder to be sure no one was listening. "At the risk of getting you in hot water, could I have a private word with you?"

Andrew glanced around. Lettie huddled over her desk, straightening her things for the night. Beyond her, the receptionist was just walking out the main door.

"Of course, ma'am."

He followed her into the large inner office, and Jillian swung around to face him. "Andrew, what have they done to Dave Hutchins? I've heard rumors that he's been fired because he violated some protocol rule."

"No. He hasn't been fired."

"On leave, then?"

"No. Well, yes, he was, but he's back now. He's just . . . They're making him push paper at the office. I heard today they might let him work on the investigation again, under Millbridge's supervision. They need him badly. I wouldn't ask Carl about it, though, if I were you."

"He and Dave don't get along."

"They're all right, but . . ." Andrew frowned. "None of us like this, Governor, but the colonel insisted."

Jillian studied his face. "Sit down for a minute. That is . . . if you dare."

Andrew cracked a smile. "If I can make a suggestion, ma'am, how about we talk in the car? It's just me today, but Ryan Mills will meet us at the Blaine House."

She nodded. "Excellent idea."

A security guard helped Andrew check the parking area before Jillian went out the back door to the vehicle.

"Tell me quick," she said as soon as Andrew was in the driver's seat. "We only have a minute."

"Apparently someone told the brass that you cried on Dave's shoulder the night you found your office had been ransacked, and implied there was more to it. That your relationship with Dave is . . . That's it's gone a lot further than that."

She sucked in a breath. "Who?"

Andrew hesitated. "I can't say for sure. I'd hate to name the wrong person."

"But it was someone who was there that Friday night?"

"Had to be. Or someone they blabbed to." He put the vehicle in gear and eased toward Capitol

Street. "We're all angry that they're doing this to Dave, but we can't do anything about it. Except freeze out the person we think did it."

Jillian pondered that. She'd noticed a distinct lack of camaraderie among the security team this week. "You know it's not true, don't you? There's never been any inappropriate conduct between Dave and me."

"Of course there hasn't. But tell that to the colonel."

Jillian pursed her lips as Andrew turned onto Grove Street. "Maybe I will."

SIXTEEN

Jillian brooded too much. She knew that, but she couldn't stop. In the last week of April, the weather broke. The days were longer and warmer, and the huge snow banks in the corners of parking lots disappeared. She tried to carry optimism into her professional and personal spheres. As she left the office a week later, she considered asking Lettie to set up a meeting with Colonel Smith. Dave shouldn't suffer for something he didn't do. Just because one of his colleagues saw him comforting her during a moment of stress, he shouldn't be in danger of losing his job.

But maybe an official meeting wasn't such a good idea. If she made this state business, it might become public. If the media got hold of it . . .

She'd invited Joe Armstrong to have dinner with her that evening. Seeing him always buoyed her spirits. Perhaps she would ask him for advice—it couldn't hurt to talk to a friend.

"I had no idea what you were going through," the old man said over coffee after dinner. "You say this officer has been disciplined, and there was nothing to it?"

"Well . . ." She smiled sheepishly. "I like him, Joe. I can't deny that. But he's never taken advantage of that fact. He's always the perfect gentleman."

"Wait a minute. Was he the one in charge the night we went to the concert?"

"Yes, Dave Hutchins."

"I remember him. I liked him, too. Told me about his hunting trip up in the Allagash last fall."

Jillian smiled at Joe's selective memory. "I suppose people see something in my face when I look at him. And that night, when I found my computer had been compromised—well, I cried a little. Not a big, messy breakdown, but . . . Joe, I think maybe one of the other officers saw him hug me, but it wasn't . . ." She sighed.

"It was just a brotherly hug?"

Jillian hung her head. "No. It was more than that. But it was far less than what's been implied. He was comforting that night. I needed that. If you'd been there, I'd have run to you, no doubt." She frowned, remembering how safe she'd felt in the circle of Dave's arms. There was no comparison to a consoling hug from Joe. "But if someone were jealous of his position or—"

"Or jealous of you?" Joe eyed her keenly.

"Maybe. I've thought about it a lot. Should I call Colonel Smith in to talk it over? Someone told Dave's boss he was involved with me, and the colonel suspended him. He's back at work now, I guess, but that's in his record. No officer should be punished for something he didn't do."

Joe sipped his coffee and set the cup down. "That might not be such a good idea, Jillian."

"No?"

Joe cocked his head to one side. "Jumping in to defend him might make you seem a bit overly concerned."

"I suppose it could."

He nodded. "Don't give cause for more gossip."

"I was afraid you'd say that. I only want to help him."

"Of course. But the more you meddle in it, the more his boss will think you care."

"Well, I do care."

Joe smiled. "Of course you do. But think, my dear. If the media tore into this story, what would become of that man?"

Jillian threw herself into her work and saw several of her proposals approved by the legislature during the next two weeks. She rarely heard Dave's name mentioned. Occasionally she asked Stephanie about him, when she was certain they would not be overheard. Stephanie obliged her, and Jillian was grateful.

One evening the second week of May she returned to the Blaine House exhausted. The double guard at the mansion remained in place, but she wondered if it was still necessary. She'd crisscrossed the state on official business, without any threatening incidents. Carl Millbridge had decreased his updates to once a week, then every other week.

A knock sounded on her door just as Jillian pulled on a thick blue fleece bathrobe.

"Who is it?"

"Naomi."

"If you were anyone else, I wouldn't want to be seen right now."

Naomi came in and sat down on the end of the queen-size bed.

"How are you doing?" Jillian sat down at her dressing table and reached for her hairbrush. "Seems like we haven't talked in ages."

"I know." Naomi met her gaze in the mirror. "I miss you. Are you okay? You look tired."

Jillian scrunched up her face. "Thanks. I am, but I'm getting a lot done."

"I'll say. I've had to read about it in the papers, though. Health care, school funding, alternative energy studies . . ." She hesitated, then pleaded, "Jill, let's go away for a bit."

"What do you mean?" Halfway into a brush stroke, Jillian stopped. "Like . . . a vacation?"

"Why not? Take a week off. You haven't had more than a day off since New Year's. We could take a cruise in the Caribbean."

"That's just plain silly." Jillian started brushing again.

"No, I'm serious. We could book under different names. No one would recognize you."

Jillian chortled. "Oh, sure. I could wear a wig and sunglasses. Naomi, I can't leave now. Besides, people would think that was frivolous. They'd be prying into my bank statements and implying I used state money to pay for it."

"I knew you'd say no." Naomi sounded disappointed.

Jillian swiveled to look directly at her. "Maybe we could do a weekend together sometime." She studied her friend's tight expression. "What have you been doing these past few weeks? I know I've neglected you horribly."

"I've gone home a few times." Naomi shrugged. "I had a couple of dates."

"With Beth's cousin?" Jillian asked. "I thought you stopped seeing him."

"I did. We just weren't on the same track. I've had a couple of other dates." Naomi laughed and pushed her hair back from her face. "I met one of the Capitol security guys, and he asked me out."

"Do you like him?"

"He's okay. But he hasn't called me again."

"Maybe he's just playing it cool."

Naomi bit her lower lip and studied the rug, then looked up to meet Jillian's gaze. "The truth is, when we went out, he just wanted to talk about you. What you're 'really' like."

Jillian caught her breath. "You mean . . . personal stuff?"

"Don't worry. I didn't tell him anything. But I figured out pretty fast that he only wanted to take me out to pump me for information. Don't get me started on the reporter from the Portland paper."

"A reporter asked you questions about me?" Jillian's voice squeaked as she spoke.

Naomi sighed and patted her arm. "I told you. I didn't give away anything. I don't want repeat dates with jerks that badly."

"You have to be careful."

"I know that."

Jillian nodded slowly. "Okay. I'll trust your discretion."

"Thanks. So I'll let you in on a secret. Remember I told you that Sean introduced me to a friend of his in Portland?"

"Yeah. Jack Something-or-other."

Naomi nodded. "I'm going out with him next Saturday."

Jillian arched her eyebrows. "First date with him?"

"Yeah. He called me a couple of times, but I didn't want to say yes until I had definitely ended things with Sean. I finally said I'd see him if he came up here. I'm not driving to Portland to meet him." She stood and stretched. "Guess

I'd better get to bed. You look like you could use about ten hours of sleep."

"Thanks!" Jillian tossed a pillow at her, and Naomi caught it, grinning.

"Oh, no. No pillow fights tonight." She laid it gently on the end of the bed. "I've got a full day tomorrow, too. They've put me in charge of scheduling all the public tours now. I'll see you at breakfast."

"Hey, wait," Jillian said. "Do you like what you're doing here?"

"It's okay. It's a lot different from the law office. Sometimes I feel as though I ought to be doing something more significant. I did talk to the administrative assistant, hence my new assignment with the tours."

"But . . . you're happy here?"

"Of course."

"Naomi, I'm sorry I've neglected you lately. You're my oldest and best friend. You know that, don't you?"

Naomi looked at her for a long moment. "I don't know. If your mom had never babysat me, do you think we would have been friends? Sometimes I wonder, why did you bring me here to share all this? Is it true friendship, or just habit?"

Stunned, Jillian stared at her. "I'm sorry you think that."

"It's not that I don't appreciate all you've done

for me. Because of you, I've gotten to do things I never would have done otherwise, and I've met people I surely wouldn't have. But sometimes I wonder, without you, who would I be?"

Jillian stood slowly and reached toward her. "If you want to find another job, that's okay. Or I could talk to the administrative assistant and see if she could turn more responsibility over to you. Maybe you can do some of the clerking, or . . . well, I don't know, but, Naomi, I do care about you. Please don't think that I don't value our friendship."

Naomi pressed her lips together and nodded. "Okay. Thanks."

"Keep me posted on how things go with Jack."

"I will." Naomi smiled, closing the door softly behind her.

Jillian stood looking at the door and feeling her heart crumble. *Lord, she's lonely. Please forgive me for not being a good friend to Naomi. And show me what I can do about it. I certainly can't take off on a cruise.* She puffed out a breath. She couldn't even blow an afternoon at the mall with her friend.

She did need a break, though. The Memorial Day holiday would come in a couple of weeks. The legislature would take a long weekend, though their session wouldn't be over. Most of the senators and representatives would spend the holidays in their home districts. Jillian wondered if she could take a three-day hiatus, as well.

She'd have to go where not many people would see her. A plan began to form in her mind. She hadn't gotten out into the wilds of Maine for months. She yearned to go visit some wilderness areas. Why not do it? A canoe trip. She hadn't been on one since Brendon died. She smiled as she ran the brush through her hair again. It would be the perfect getaway.

"A quiet weekend canoeing in the Allagash to escape the pressures of this office. That's all I'm asking."

Colonel Smith frowned and balanced his hat on his knee. "Ma'am, I know you've been working very hard, and you certainly deserve some time off. But I don't think you understand the difficulties we'd face if we did what you're proposing."

"We haven't had any serious incidents since late February. I've felt lately that we're wasting taxpayers' money by keeping such a heavy security team on duty all the time."

"How do we know the reverse isn't true, ma'am? That we haven't had any problems in the last three months because we've been vigilant?"

She sat back with a sigh. "All right, so send all the EPU officers you want. But we won't tell anyone where we're going until the last minute—not even my guests."

"And who might that be?" Smith asked.

"I thought I'd take Naomi Plante and two couples from my old law firm. Eric and Margaret Harris, and Jon and Bette Scribner."

"Hmm." Smith's eyebrows drew together. "Six people to protect. We'd have to send at least four officers, I guess. Six would be better, if we can find that many who qualify for a wilderness trip. That's a lot of gear."

Jillian relaxed in her chair. He was seriously considering her idea. "If the Scribners and the Harrises are able to go, I'm sure they'd be happy to supply their own gear. I have a canoe, and so do Eric and Margaret Harris."

Smith pulled out a pocket notebook and jotted a few notes. "I'm not saying yes, but I'll run it by the public safety officer." He wagged a finger at her. "Don't say anything to your friends yet. I'll let you know by tomorrow if it's a go. If it is, we'll set it up and make all the arrangements. I do *not* want this leaking out."

"Thank you!" Jillian couldn't help grinning as they said good-bye. If it worked out, the trip would give her just what she needed: a couple of days detached from the city and the machinations of government. Physical exercise and the soothing effect of nature. Time with friends. Just a peaceful, rustic getaway.

The thought of renewing her girlhood camaraderie with Naomi eased her heart. They'd have a chance for a long, private talk on the weekend trip, and they could rebuild the closeness they'd lost.

She tried not to think of Dave and how much fun a canoeing trip would be with him along. But she wouldn't ever mention his name to the colonel. It would only feed his belief that Dave had broken regulations and pursued an unethical relationship with her. She had to admit, however, that a part of her was hoping against hope that somehow Dave would be one of the guards assigned to her trip. And not just because he was good at his job.

SEVENTEEN

As Dave sat in the duty room typing his daily report on Monday, he felt someone watching him. He glanced up and stopped typing. Lieutenant Wilson leaned in the doorway, frowning as he looked at him. When Dave caught his eye, the lieutenant straightened and walked toward him.

"Dave, I need a private word with you."

Dave exhaled slowly. This couldn't be good. It never was. Suspension? More rumors? Something worse? For weeks he'd kept away from the Blaine House and the Capitol building, doing mundane research and clerk's duties—background checks on people invited to events where the governor would be present, computerizing old records that hadn't been touched in twenty years. The closest he'd come to Jillian was taking the SUV to have the oil changed. He'd quit watching the local news. Her frequent appearances on the broadcasts only made his heart ache.

He followed Wilson to his office. The lieutenant closed the door and gestured toward a chair. He sat down behind his desk and picked up a paper clip.

"You got plans for the holiday weekend?"

Dave stared at him. "You got an assignment for me?"

"For real. Overtime, even."

"Okay, I'm in."

"You don't even know what it is yet."

Dave shrugged. "It's got to be more exciting than what I've been doing for the last few weeks."

Wilson nodded, unfolding the paper clip and twisting it into a letter *S*. "Look, you can't say anything to anyone. This is hush-hush. If you've got plans, that's fine. I'll get someone else. Though we're a bit hard up for manpower right now."

"I heard Mike Hewitt broke his leg yesterday."

"Yeah. That's exactly why we need you." Wilson cleared his throat. "Okay, well, I had to get you cleared for this, but the colonel and I agreed, better you than one of the rookies we just hired. I had Mike signed up for the trip, but—"

"He obviously can't go now."

"Right." Wilson tossed the paper clip down and rubbed his eyebrows. "Stupid motorcycle accident. I keep telling you guys not to do extreme sports on your days off. Anyway. So, you're in?"

"You said *trip*. Where am I going?"

Wilson chuckled. "Can't tell you. It's a mystery jaunt. Only Ryan Mills and I know so far."

"Ryan's in on this?" Dave sat a little straighter. The young detective had been on Blaine House duty since the inauguration. His curiosity was keener than ever now. "What's going on, Lieutenant?"

Wilson's lips twitched for a moment before he responded. "This is strictly on the Q.T. The governor needs a minivacation."

Dave arched his eyebrows, but said nothing. He couldn't believe that Wilson meant for him to be in Jillian's proximity again.

"Hey, I tried everyone else who's eligible. Most of the others never held a canoe paddle in their lives."

"Canoe paddle?" Dave's adrenaline jump-started an erratic pulse pattern. The one time he and Jillian discussed canoeing, she'd said she didn't like white water. Half a dozen possible destinations came to mind. Most likely northern Maine. He grinned at Wilson. "Who else is going?"

"Two of the governor's old law partners and their spouses. You've probably met Margaret Harris and Jon Scribner?"

"Yes. Is that it?"

"Besides the EPU, yeah. Governor Goff invited Naomi Plante, but she'd already made other plans and won't be back until Sunday. The governor thought about postponing the trip, but the others could make it, and she didn't know when she'd have the chance again, so we've gone ahead and made arrangements. No one will know the ultimate destination until after you leave Friday afternoon."

"Who are the other officers onboard?"

"Penny—she's got a little experience kayaking and canoeing. And Jerry Knott. He's only been with us a few months, but like I said, I'm desperate. And he grew up on Moosehead Lake."

Dave nodded. "Good." He didn't know Jerry well, but what he'd seen of the young man he liked. "It's a good team."

"Think so?"

"Sure. Ryan's in charge?"

"Yes, but you have more wilderness experience. I sounded him out on how he'd feel about us tapping you after Mike broke his leg, and he's good with it. He'll be responsible for the governor's safety. You'll handle the logistics of the trip—moving the gear, making sure your campsite is safe. And you'll report in by radio regularly. Penny and Jerry will each be assigned to one of the couples. Of course, if it comes right down to it, you're all there for the governor. But if the Harrises or the Scribners need help, Penny and Jerry will handle it."

"Sounds good."

"The lawyers have to return late Sunday, but the governor wants to stay out until Monday. One of you will have to escort the Harrises and

Scribners to the jumping-off point to make sure they get out safely. Not Penny—she doesn't have enough canoeing experience." Wilson sighed and slapped the folder shut. "I wish we could send a couple more men, but we're stretching the budget as it is."

"We'll be fine." Dave smiled at him. "Thanks for giving me the chance."

"Colonel Smith doesn't like it, but the truth is, I leaned on the officer who turned you in, and the allegations have been withdrawn."

Dave's heart lurched. "Really?"

"Yes. I can't give you the details, and the colonel is still skeptical, but if you behave yourself, maybe you'll be off his bad list after this."

"I wish."

Wilson shrugged. "Hey, you got a raw deal. But if anyone asks, I never said that."

Friday evening's caravan included three vehicles. Ryan drove the SUV carrying Jillian and the Harrises, while Penny rode with Jon and Bette Scribner in their Jeep. Dave and Jerry followed in a Chevy Blazer borrowed from the Department of Inland Fisheries and Wildlife. It lacked the bulletproof glass and other features of the SUV in which the governor traveled, but was more practical and less conspicuous than the Lincoln would have been. It was loaded with gear and carried a canoe on top, as did the other two vehicles.

Dave hummed along with the radio. He'd have to be careful about his contact with Jillian, but he couldn't deny the anticipation that rose in his heart. Ryan had told the security team their destination only minutes before they left the Blaine House. Instead of Aroostook County, they headed for northern Somerset, where a small, secluded lake bounded by paper company land nestled between mountains.

They rolled through Caratunk about seven o'clock. The sun dropped behind the distant pines and spruces, and when they arrived at their overnight stop an hour later, the light had faded. A snug cabin, sided with knotty pine boards, squatted on the verge of a small, calm lake.

"This camp belongs to Fish and Wildlife," Ryan said as they climbed out of the vehicles. A woodpile leaned against one side of the cabin, and an open porch with a rough railing jutted out before the front door. "We'll have it easy tonight. A gas stove to cook on, bunks to sleep in. In the morning, we'll paddle the length of the lake and take the river at the other end a few miles up to the next pond. There's one campsite on the far end of it. We'll start roughing it there."

"Great," Eric said.

"We get a lake to ourselves?" Jillian asked.

"That's right. A paper company owns it, and the only campsite is waiting for us. No one will bother you, Governor."

Jillian exhaled and hugged herself. "Thank you." She looked around at Penny, Dave and Jerry. "Thank you *all*. I appreciate your giving up the holiday weekend to make this possible for me and my friends."

They all smiled. Dave thought Jillian looked beautiful in dark pants, a striped T-shirt, zippered navy sweatshirt and hiking boots. Her golden hair was pulled back in a ponytail. He made himself look away before the others caught him staring.

"Hey, we're having fun, too," Jerry assured her.

Margaret clapped her hands. "So! What have we got for supper? I'm starved."

"Steaks," Ryan said. "Let us make a quick inspection of the camp, and then you can move in."

Five minutes later, Dave and Jerry carried two coolers inside, while Eric Harris and Jon Scribner began to ferry in the sleeping bags and other gear.

Jillian, Margaret and Bette took over the kitchen with Penny. They cooked supper while the men unloaded the canoes and made preparations for an early-morning departure. Dave radioed head-quarters to tell Wilson they had arrived safely.

When Penny called the men inside, Dave told Ryan, "I'll keep watch out here while you all eat. Just save me something, okay?"

The other men went in, and Dave walked slowly

to the water's edge. Aside from the low murmur of voices from the cabin, the only sound was the sigh of a light breeze in the evergreens. A slap on the water drew his attention to a ripple spreading near one edge of the pond. Must be a beaver lodge over there near the western shore, Dave thought.

He turned and walked stealthily around the cabin, beneath the dark evergreens, then to the front again. He paced between the vehicles and looked down the access road. Leaning against the smooth trunk of a beech tree, he lifted his eyes to the glittering stars. *Lord, thank You for letting me come on this trip. Help us to keep her safe, and let her have a good time. Give her some rest, Father.*

The breeze caused gentle waves that lapped against the rocky shore. Again he made his solitary circuit of the cabin.

When he came around to the front, someone stood on the porch, leaning on the railing and looking toward the water. The golden hair told him it was Jillian, though the jacket she'd donned camouflaged her figure. His pulse picked up, but he made himself keep walking slowly, deliberately, until he was just below her. She stood above him, resting her forearms on the rail.

"Beautiful night," she said softly.

"Yes." He leaned against the porch. They stood for a long time without speaking. From inside,

Dave could hear occasional bursts of laughter and muffled voices. "How have you been?" he asked at last.

"Fine. I'm tired, but . . . I'm getting things done, Dave."

"Yes." He turned and looked up at her.

She met his gaze with the light of the newly risen moon playing over her delicate features. He ached all over.

"I've missed you," he said.

Her mouth softened into a near smile. "I was hoping that you . . . I can't believe you're actually here."

"Me either." He decided to ask what he'd wondered for the last week. "You didn't ask for me, did you?"

"No." Her laugh was like music. "I didn't know you were coming until today. I tried not to show my shock, but Bette's been needling me a little. She must have seen something in the way I looked at you."

A warm glow started deep in Dave's chest. "Lieutenant Wilson said they were desperate. One of the men who should be here broke his leg. The lieutenant arranged it, but I've got to be on my best behavior."

She nodded soberly. "I understand. But we'll have times to talk, won't we? Times like this?"

He hesitated. "I hope so."

"I've missed talking to you more than anything, Dave." She bent toward him and extended her hand. He reached up and took it, enveloping her small, warm fingers in his clasp. Jillian exhaled and looked out over the smooth lake.

He didn't trust himself to speak. A loon laughed far down the lake. "Listen," Jillian said. "I haven't heard that sound in years."

Behind her, the cabin door opened and Ryan stepped out. Dave released her hand, quickly crossing his arms.

"All right, ma'am?" Ryan asked.

"Yes, thank you." Jillian glanced over her shoulder at him. "Detective Hutchins is here, too, so I'm safe."

Ryan stepped forward, but stopped when he caught sight of Dave standing below them. He nodded, and Dave returned the acknowledgment. "I'll make another round. See you later."

"Did you want to stay out here for a while, ma'am?" Ryan asked. "I could bring you a chair."

"No, I think I'll go in. It's getting a little chilly."

Dave heard the door close behind them as he rounded the corner by the woodpile. His heart still hammered. He ran his fingertips over his scratchy cheek, remembering how guilelessly she'd reached for him. The suspension and the weeks of dejection and loneliness—that one moment was worth it all.

EIGHTEEN

The early sunlight sparkled on the water as they set off on Saturday morning. Jillian paddled steadily, reveling in the glory of the day. Her muscles would ache tomorrow for sure, but she didn't care. She didn't mind that Dave was in another canoe, either. With Ryan and Jerry, she guided their craft along swiftly, flipping water playfully at Jon and Bette as her canoe glided past theirs. The race was on. Dave's paddle dove deep below the surface as he helped the Scribners try to regain the lead.

Soon Penny and the Harrises joined the competition, and all three canoes raced toward the far end of the lake with the paddlers laughing and trading good-natured jabs.

"Hey, Bette," Jillian called across to her friend, "you paddle like a girl."

Bette hiked her chin up. "You talk big, Goff."

"Cat fight!" Jon hit the water with the broadside of his blade, sending a shower of water toward Jillian, but her canoe was moving so fast that the splash hit Jerry.

By the time they reached the landing place at the lake's tip, all of them had slowed down, fighting for each stroke. Dave and the Scribners' canoe hit the gravel beach first. Jon stood in the bow and crowed, hefting his paddle over his head.

Jerry laughed. "Big buncha kids."

"Oh, yeah." Jillian turned to smile at him. "Get 'em away from the law books, and they can really cut loose."

Dave built a fire on the beach, and they took their time fixing hot coffee and eating sandwiches, raw vegetables and cookies.

As the others finished their coffee, Jillian rose and walked along the shore, stooping now and then to pick up a dry stick. When she'd gone perhaps fifty yards, she swung around to look back. Ryan pulled up two paces behind her.

"Sorry, ma'am. I know you like your privacy, but . . ."

"That's okay, Ryan. I'm getting used to it." She looked toward the woods that came to the verge of the lake, the vast blueness of sky and water. "This is just what I needed."

"I'm glad we could give it to you." He looked over his shoulder. "It's probably not a good idea for you to get too far away from the others."

"All right." She turned back and walked beside him. "We're going up the river this afternoon, right?"

"Yes, ma'am. It will be a tough pull up the stream, and it's a rocky stretch. We'll be fighting a swift current, but I don't think it will take more than an hour to get to the other lake."

She considered that. "Do you think it's better to rest a little longer here, or to get to the campsite and set up early?"

"Whatever you'd like, ma'am."

"Oh, stop it." She laughed. "You're in charge on this trip, so forget my office. I left that in Augusta."

"Well, then, I'd say let's head upstream," Ryan said. "If we need to, we'll have time to portage. Once we're at our campsite, you can rest or fish or do whatever you want."

"Okay, let's go." As they walked back toward the campfire, she noticed Dave gazing at her. Jillian smiled, and his sober expression at once lifted into one of expectation. In this setting, he was more handsome than ever. His olive-drab shirt, with the sleeves rolled above the elbows, reminded her that Dave had a past in the military. She sent up a prayer of thanks that he had come home safely to the achingly beautiful wilderness of Maine.

Ryan quickly organized the packing of the gear. Jillian filled a pan full of lake water to douse the fire and met Dave at the fire pit as he laid a small pile of kindling nearby for the next campers.

"Hi." Immediately, she thought how silly that sounded. They'd been within yards of each other all morning, but hadn't spoken to each other.

"Hello."

The memory of his gentle touch the previous evening sent a wave of blood to her cheeks. "Is your brother still in Iraq?"

His eyebrows arched. "Yes."

"Sorry. That wasn't really out of the blue. I was thinking about him. About . . . all our troops. And about you being home. I'm glad you're here and in one piece."

"Thanks. He's got three months to go."

"I'll keep praying for him."

"I appreciate that." Dave's deep brown eyes lingered on her face.

"Are you ready?" Ryan called from near the water.

Penny, Margaret and Eric had shoved off and were paddling toward the mouth of the stream.

Dave threw her a quick smile and went to join Jon and Bette.

Jillian took her place in the center canoe with Ryan and Jerry. The orders must be followed—Jillian in the middle of the pack at all times. She didn't mind, though it meant Penny and the Harrises were the first to see the moose that stood in the water up to its flanks, chewing on aquatic weeds. The giant stared balefully at them as they paddled past. Jillian got her camera out in time to snap a couple of pictures.

Ryan was right—the trip upstream was tough

but exhilarating. They reached their destination around three o'clock. Jillian and Penny would share a tent, and Jillian insisted they could erect it themselves.

"Wouldn't want you guys to think I'm helpless outside the office," she told Jerry.

Twenty minutes later, she wished she'd kept her mouth shut. The tent was large enough to sleep six—and needed about as many people to raise it.

"Hold it," Penny called. Jillian strained to keep one of the poles steady while Penny stretched the material out. The whole thing came loose and billowed down over her. She batted at the dark nylon, laughing as it folded about her.

"Have you ladies had enough?" Dave's deep voice asked. "I wouldn't want to barge in where I'm not wanted, but it seems to me you could use some extra manpower."

"Hey, I'm not the one who said we could do it alone," Penny retorted. "Get over here!"

"You sure?" Ryan asked.

"If you ever want to see the governor again, you'd better help me get this stupid tent off her."

The others laughed, but Jillian heard Ryan's quiet voice close by saying, "Easy, Penny, you're not supposed to say the *G* word, remember? We're just a bunch of friends on a camping trip."

"Oh, right," Penny muttered. "Friends carrying guns and keeping watch 24/7."

Bright sunlight reached Jillian as they lifted the tent off her.

"Thanks, guys." She smiled at them. "I admit I was overly ambitious."

"That's okay," Jerry assured her. "We enjoyed the entertainment."

Jillian helped them finish the job, while Margaret and Bette set up their camp kitchen. After supper, she and Margaret cleaned up while the others prepared their tackle for an hour of fishing before sunset.

"You hit the jackpot on handsome security guards." Margaret grinned at her as she scrubbed the frying pan.

Jillian shrugged and smiled. "They're great guys. I don't know Jerry very well—he's new. But Ryan's been with me since January, and Dave . . ." She hesitated, not sure how to describe her nonrelationship with the rugged EPU officer.

"You mean he's the one?" Margaret stared at her wide-eyed.

Jillian caught her breath. "Margaret! Hush. There was nothing to that. It was a stupid rumor, is all."

Her friend eyed her sagely. "But you wish there *was* something to it."

Jillian glanced toward where Dave patrolled between the tents and the forest. "Please be careful. If you say something like that in Augusta, it could cost him his job. He's done nothing unethical. Nothing."

Margaret's eyes narrowed as she followed Jillian's gaze. "He's gorgeous."

Jillian felt her cheeks flush. "Will you stop?"

"What's he doing on this expedition? I thought there was some disciplinary action."

"Dave was the officer who briefed me on the investigations of the attempted shootings, nothing more. But someone started a vicious rumor, and he was suspended for a short time and placed on other duties."

"I repeat, why is he here?"

Jillian sighed. "He's a last-minute replacement for some poor officer who broke his leg."

Margaret studied her face. "Are you uncomfortable having him around?"

"No," Jillian said quickly. Margaret's immediate smile caused her flush to deepen. "I mean . . ." Jillian looked toward Dave again. In his wide circuit of the camp, he'd made a loop and was now headed back toward them. "He's not supposed to have contact with me, but—"

"Even on this trip?"

"No. Yes. I don't know." Jillian shook her head. "No one said anything to me about it. I didn't even know he was coming. Ryan told me about two hours before we left the Blaine House. But I know Dave is determined not to raise any suspicions this weekend." She glanced again toward him. He was only a dozen yards away. "Can we please not talk about this now?"

"Sure." Margaret put the frying pan in the box of cookware. "I guess we'll need this again for breakfast. What about the food boxes and coolers? We can't leave them out tonight."

Dave was close enough to hear her last remark, and he stepped toward them briskly. "That's right, Mrs. Harris. We're in bear country. Ryan and I will cache the food containers."

Margaret looked up at him with a broad smile. "Hi, Dave. Please call me Margaret. No formality on this trip."

"Okay." He grinned back, and Jillian looked away before he could turn his endearing smile on her. She would melt if he did. "We plan to anchor a canoe off shore with the coolers in it. It should be calm tonight, so I don't think there's any danger of losing our rations to the deep."

Jillian felt him watching her.

"Are you going fishing?" she asked.

"No, it's my turn to . . . stay alert." He chuckled, and she made the mistake of looking into his eyes this time. She felt as though a bear had come along in broad daylight and squeezed the air out of her lungs.

"Oh. Somebody's got to, I guess."

Margaret giggled as though Jillian had said something extremely witty. She picked up her wet dish cloth. "I'm going to hang this on that bush over there to dry."

Jillian watched her walk away, feeling a rush of panic. Margaret had obviously left them alone on purpose. Last night, with Dave standing below her in the moonlight as she leaned on the porch railing, everything had seemed right. But now, in brilliant sunlight . . .

"I thought Ryan was my watchdog for the weekend," she said.

"He is, but since everything's quiet, we agreed he could go fishing with the others and I'd keep an eye on things until dark. Then we'll swap off a double guard all night."

"That's a lot of trouble for the unit."

He shrugged. "We're enjoying it. I should scout around some more, though. Why don't you go fishing with the rest?"

"I . . ."

"Don't tell me you don't have a license."

She chuckled and pushed back a stray lock of hair. "I do. Ryan got it for me when he got the fire permits. Maybe I will." But neither of them moved.

Margaret called from near the Harrises' tent, "Hey, Jill, did you bring a swimsuit?"

Jillian stared at her. "You're joking. Didn't you feel that water? It's ice cold."

"Yeah, I'm kidding." Margaret ducked into the tent.

Jillian looked up at Dave again. His mouth twitched, as though holding back a laugh was major work.

"I'll see you later," she said softly, smiling at him.

"Right." He turned and walked toward the beached canoes.

The next morning, Jillian woke early. Penny's regular breathing told her the officer still slept, and Jillian was glad. She felt a smidgen of guilt for causing four people to lose the better part of a night's sleep to make sure she was safe.

The rising sun bathed the tent wall with glowing light, and she rolled out of her sleeping bag. At the end of her air mattress she found her duffel bag and boots, and in a matter of minutes she crept out of the tent and zipped the flap down. Dave crouched at the fire pit, feeding a small blaze, and she walked over and extended her hands toward the flames.

He looked up at her and smiled. "You're up early."

"Actually, I'm usually up about this time. I guess you're on duty."

He nodded. "Ryan and me. He's off down the beach."

Jillian could just see Ryan walking slowly along between the trees and the rocky shore.

"I've got the coffeepot ready to go," Dave said.

227

She picked it up from beside the woodpile. Dave lowered the metal grill over the fire and she set the pot on it. She pulled over a canvas folding chair and sat on the upwind side of the fire. Dave lingered, poking at the burning logs with a stick.

"I've been thinking a lot about Naomi," he said, not looking at her.

"Oh? I hoped she'd come with us."

"You invited her, didn't you?"

Jillian sighed and leaned back in the chair, looking out over the placid lake. "She wanted me to go on a cruise with her, and I told her I couldn't. But when I thought of a way she and I could have some fun together, she'd made other plans. I feel as though I haven't paid her much attention lately."

"You've been busy."

"I have. And I was hoping this weekend would make up for it. But she's spending the weekend with some guy she hardly knows."

His eyes widened. "Do you know anything about him?"

"His name is Jack something." She scowled, trying to remember the name. "She's only been out with him twice before this. But the real issue is that I'm not sure she's happy with her job anymore."

"She's tired of living in the Blaine House?"

Jillian pursed her lips as she considered the question. "She likes living there, but I think she's

228

bored. And she as much as said I haven't been a true friend. In fact, she hinted that our friendship is one of convenience."

"Is it?"

"I wouldn't like to think so."

Dave broke a small stick in half and dropped the pieces into the fire. "Is she a believer?"

His question struck Jillian's heart. How many people would ask her such a thing? In the political sphere, most of her acquaintances carefully avoided religious topics.

"I'm not really sure. She sometimes attends church with me, but I think it's more of a social thing."

"Wants to be seen with the governor?"

She frowned. "I hope not."

"How about when you were kids?"

Jillian shook her head. "Her family didn't go to church. She went a few times with mine. But as much as I hate to say it, she never seemed to want to talk about spiritual things, and . . ."

"What?" He looked intently into her eyes.

"I never pushed it. I was content to let it slide and figure, either she knew God or someone else would tell her." Tears welled in her eyes. "How could I know her for more than twenty years and not once sit her down and tell her what Christ did for me?"

He was quiet for a long moment, watching the flames. "Maybe the time hasn't been right yet."

He looked at her with such sympathy she was afraid she'd lose it.

"What made you think of Naomi, Dave?"

He swallowed hard. "It seems to me that Naomi is the only person who had access to your office the day your computer was compromised, other than the staff."

A tear rolled down her cheek. She swiped at it with her sleeve. "She said it wasn't her, but I've wondered." Dave looked at her in surprise. "I don't know why she'd do it, though."

Ryan was approaching the camp. He waved, and Jillian raised her arm in return. Instead of coming closer, he detoured off behind the tents.

Dave stood. "Can you think of anyone else—anyone who's made you feel uncomfortable in the last few months?"

She huffed out a sigh then shrugged. "Not really. Unless maybe Penny."

Dave raised his eyebrows.

Jillian wished she'd said nothing. She glanced toward her tent, but it was far enough away that their soft tones wouldn't carry that far. "You said uncomfortable. I didn't mean that I don't trust her."

"What's the story with Penny?" Dave asked quietly.

"Sometimes I've felt she didn't really like me." It sounded silly, and Jillian leaned toward him, eager to explain. "She's always respectful, but . . .

well, being a woman in a public position, sometimes it's hard to read other women. I wonder, does this person like me, or is she just doing her duty? And with Penny, sometimes I feel as though she's taken a personal dislike to me. Occasionally, I've thought that it might have something to do with you, Dave. With our friendship, I mean."

"Do you mean . . ."

"It seems like maybe she has feelings for you. And I'm guessing she's perceived something between you and me."

Dave nodded, not meeting her gaze.

"Do you think I'm right?"

"Let's just say that there have been times when I've questioned her motives, too. But for whatever it's worth, Jillian, there's nothing between Penny and me. Nothing," he said again, staring at her intensely.

"Here comes Ryan," she said quickly.

He smiled—the crooked heart-stopper that she'd dreamed about for months—and stood.

Jillian watched him walk away, wondering if everyone else could see the obvious. She exhaled carefully. Could she be with the man she loved without costing him his job?

Had she truly just thought of him as *the man she loved?*

She had. And a smile spread across her face that she knew would be with her the rest of the day.

NINETEEN

On Sunday afternoon, Dave and the other officers stood back while Jillian made the rounds, hugging her friends on the gravel beach.

"Thanks so much for coming. This weekend was wonderful."

Margaret returned her embrace and kissed her cheek. "Yes it was. Are you sure you want to stay out here alone tonight?"

Jillian laughed. "I'll hardly be alone. I just hate to leave this paradise a minute before I have to."

"Right. Well, catch a big trout for me." Margaret squeezed her and turned toward the canoes.

Jillian held out her arms to Jon Scribner. "Thanks for being here, Jon. I hope you had fun."

"The best, Jill. Thanks for having us along."

Bette claimed the last hug. "I wish we didn't have to leave, but Jon promised his folks we'd be at their house tomorrow morning to watch the parade with them."

Jillian crinkled up her nose. "Enjoy it. I know my critics think I should be making the rounds of the parades in different towns, but I'm taking one more day to relax."

Bette nodded. "You may not get another chance

for a while. And with all of us gone, it should be even more peaceful here tonight."

Ryan drew Dave aside. "Are you sure you'll be okay taking them down to the vehicles?"

"Sure," Dave said. "I'll get them down to the warden camp, pack them off for home and then come back here."

Ryan nodded. "I know this was part of the plan, since the legal eagles have to leave early, but I wish I could send Jerry."

Dave shook his head. "It's best this way."

Ryan's radio beeped, and he turned aside. "Bronte One, over."

The dispatcher in Augusta spoke, and Ryan walked away. Dave watched as Ryan stopped, clearly distressed.

"Are we all set?" Eric Harris called.

"Just a sec," Dave said.

Ryan walked toward him frowning. "Dave, can I talk to you?" Dave walked toward the fire pit with him, and Ryan lowered his voice. "My dad had a heart attack."

Dave laid a hand on his shoulder. "I'm sorry. Is he—"

"He's in the hospital. They're not sure he'll make it. I need to go."

"Yes, you do." Dave looked toward the others waiting on the beach. "Look, you go with the lawyers. You'll be able to call your mother on your cell phone when you get down to the warden camp. She needs you. Don't worry about us."

"But the governor—"

"She'll still have three of us tonight." Dave squeezed his shoulder. "Ryan, you need to go. The colonel will understand."

"I can't put you in charge."

Dave knew he was right. Smith would go ballistic if he learned Dave had been directly responsible for the governor at any point during the weekend. "Put Penny in charge. Jerry's too new."

"Maybe we should all go back."

"No, we'll be fine. Really."

Ryan pulled in a deep breath. "Okay. I'll call Augusta and tell them. You'll have to get Bronte down safely tomorrow."

"We will. Penny, Jerry and I can handle it. And headquarters can send another officer to meet us in the morning if they want to."

Ryan completed his radio call to Augusta while Dave switched Ryan's gear for his and explained the situation to the others. The Scribners settled in their canoe, with Ryan in the stern. Dave waded into the water, shoving them off. He glanced over at Jillian. She watched the canoeists, holding up one hand in salute. Margaret looked back and waved her paddle.

Jillian's golden hair fluttered about her face,

and her forest-green sweater and brown corduroys gave her a wholesome, athletic air. Her blue eyes reflected the clear sky and water. Dave didn't even try to stop watching her. His heart was hers. He was almost ready to consider going back into the regular state police, if that would mean he could see Jillian without repercussions. And if the governor didn't mind having a detective for a boyfriend. Would she? How would it look? Would the media make her miserable?

She turned and smiled at him, and his face flushed as if she had just read his mind or something. Silly. She had no idea what he was thinking.

"You'll miss your friends," he said.

"Yes. You three will have to keep me company tonight so I won't be lonesome." She turned to Penny and Jerry. "I'm not nearly as good a cook as Margaret. Will someone help me cook those trout tonight?"

"Sure." Penny stepped toward her. "Let's make sure we've got plenty of firewood."

"Don't go far," Dave said.

Penny made a face at him. "We won't. But we'll be fine." She patted her side, where her pistol and portable radio rested.

Dave said to Jerry, "What do you say we tighten up the camp? Pull our tent in closer to theirs."

Jerry nodded. "Good idea. And we need to

decide how the three of us will split up the watch tonight."

By the time the men had the camp battened down to their satisfaction, Penny and Jillian had gathered enough wood to last all night, provided Dave would chop up a small fallen tree they'd dragged into the clearing. He went at it without complaint. As he worked, the tantalizing smell of frying fish wafted across the camp.

Jerry approached as he stacked the last of his split logs on the woodpile.

"There's a boat at the far end of the lake."

Dave straightened and squinted, but he couldn't see anything. Without speaking, he ducked into the men's tent and grabbed his binoculars. He and Jerry walked down to the beach together.

Dave looked and then handed Jerry the binoculars. "Anyone can come up here. Just because there's only one campsite doesn't mean they can't fish on the lake."

Jerry adjusted the glasses. "They seem to be sitting down there near the outlet. I think I see a fishing pole."

Dave called Ryan on the radio, hoping he had some information for them. Ryan answered, saying he was helping the lawyers load their Jeep.

"Yeah, we saw a couple of guys in the boat at the bottom of the stream," Ryan reported. "Didn't think they'd go all the way up there."

"Let's keep an eye on them," Dave said to Jerry.

"What do you want to do if they come up here?" Jerry asked.

"Put Jillian in her tent and shoot the breeze until they leave."

Jerry pressed his lips together and handed the binoculars back.

"And don't say the word 'governor,' " Dave added.

"We'd better tell Penny."

"We should tell them both." Dave looked toward the fire pit. "Jillian needs to be ready if they come closer."

Jillian wished she'd gone back with her friends. Dave's announcement that someone else was on the lake made her stomach churn, the way it had after the sniper shot at her in the Blaine House yard. Dave walked down the shore with a pair of binoculars around his neck. She could just see him sitting on a rock a hundred yards away, watching the far end of the lake.

The sun lowered, and with the chilly evening air, an uneasy mood descended. Penny pitched in on the cleanup without her former perkiness.

As the shadows lengthened into twilight, Dave returned to the camp. "They headed down the river about twenty minutes ago. I waited to make sure they were gone. I think Jerry and I should paddle down there and take a look around. Would you feel safer tonight if we did?"

"Would you?" Jillian countered.

Dave gritted his teeth. "To be honest, yeah."

"I'll go," Penny said. "Jerry should stay here with Jillian. Two women in the wilderness would look more vulnerable than a man and a woman."

Dave eyed her pensively, then nodded. "Agreed."

"You two be careful," Jillian said.

"I'm sure there's no reason for alarm," Dave said. "Just a couple of avid fishermen who've now headed home."

Still, it was enough to put them all on edge. Jerry prowled the camp as dusk deepened. Twice Jillian heard him speaking into his radio. She loaded wood onto the fire until the flames burned high, then poured herself a mug of coffee. She sat watching the blaze and praying silently.

An hour later, Dave and Penny paddled quietly up to the shore and beached the canoe. Jillian set her mug down and hurried to them, and Jerry came from patrolling the edge of the woods.

"All clear," Dave said.

Penny hopped out of the canoe and unfastened her lifejacket. "It was dark by the time we got down there, but they're gone."

"We looked down the stream," Dave said. "Couldn't see any lights or anything."

They sat by the fire for another hour, Penny taking the early watch. Dave and Jerry told a few stories about their experiences as police officers, and Jillian gradually relaxed. But the easy camaraderie had an edge. She never quite forgot that she had to be careful, or that the three sharing the camp with her had come along only to protect her.

Jerry pushed the light button on his watch. "Guess it's time for me to relieve Penny." He stood and stretched.

"Are you tired?" Dave asked Jillian.

"I think I could stay awake for a s'more."

"Did someone say s'mores?" Penny called as she came toward them out of the darkness. "I'll get the marshmallows."

They sat up another half hour. Jillian made a s'more for Jerry and called him over when his patrol brought him near the campfire.

"I think I'd better quit," Penny said. "I am sugared out."

"Me too. You want any more, Dave?" Jillian held up the bag of marshmallows.

"No, I'm good."

She put the bag in the cooler and turned the clasp. "Do we need to float the cooler in the canoe tonight?"

Dave rose. "I'll take care of it."

Jillian yawned. "I think I'll turn in." She moved her chair away from the fireside. "Thanks for doing this with me. It's been really fun."

"It's the best three days on the job I've had all year," Penny said.

Jillian smiled. "Glad to hear it." She nodded at Dave. "See you in the morning."

She turned toward the tent and a sudden thought popped into her mind. "I remembered that name, Dave. Kendall," she said.

Dave swung around and stared at her. "What?"

"Jack Kendall. Sorry, it just came to me. That's Naomi's new boyfriend."

Dave's expression froze. "Are you sure?"

The look in Dave's eyes sent chills up Jillian's spine. "Yes. Why? Do you—"

He set the cooler down. "Penny, stay with her. I need to call HQ."

"What is it?" Jillian stared at his stony face and her pulse thudded. "You know him?"

"He's Tanger's son." Dave already had the radio in his hand.

"How can that be?" Jillian gasped.

Penny hurried to her side. "Roderick Tanger had two children, but his wife divorced him and remarried ages ago. Long before you put him in prison."

"So his children's stepfather could have adopted them."

Penny nodded. "Have you met this man? Did Naomi ever bring him to the Blaine House?"

"No." Jillian's stomach lurched. How did she know what Naomi did while she was gone all day? As a resident, Naomi had permission to bring personal guests into the house. "If she asked him to come, wouldn't the EPU do a background on him?"

"Yes, unless she got around that somehow."

Jillian seized Penny's arm. "Let's not jump to conclusions. He may not be the same person. And Naomi wouldn't date him if she knew he was related to Tanger."

Penny held her gaze. "Do you know that for sure?"

Jillian felt light-headed. She looked over at Dave.

"That's correct. Jack or John Kendall," he was saying into the radio. "We need to know where he is. Pick him up."

"Come on," Penny said. "Let's get ready for bed."

With shaking hands, Jillian stowed her boots and snuggled into her sleeping bag fully clothed. Penny lay still beside her. Jillian began to pray silently. *Lord, calm my spirit. Keep us safe. Help me to quit worrying. And whatever happens, protect Naomi. Draw her close to You, Lord.*

Dave and Jerry's low voices drifted on the quiet breeze, along with the gentle slap of waves on the rocks and the rustling of the pine branches. Jillian concentrated on relaxing, muscle by

241

muscle. In spite of the coffee she'd downed, she started to slip into sleep.

Crack!

She sat bolt upright in the darkness, her heart crashing around in her chest.

Dave threw himself to the ground and listened.

He couldn't take a risk by calling out to Jerry. The stillness was broken only by the wind and the waves.

Dave rose on his knees and looked carefully all around the camp. Only a couple of minutes ago, he'd seen Jerry go silently toward the back of the tents to continue his patrol. Was Penny still in the tent with Jillian?

What if she'd slipped into the woods to ambush them?

He hated the fact that he'd even had the thought. And yet Jillian had felt ill at ease with Penny, and Dave had recognized Penny's jealousy. On this trip, she'd seemed to have gotten past that, but what if she'd simply learned to hide it well?

He scurried toward the women's tent, bending low. Soft rustlings came from within.

"Penny?" he called softly.

"Yeah. What's going on?"

Dave breathed again. "Gunshot. I'm not sure where Jerry is."

"I know I'm technically in charge here, but I'll

defer to you," Penny said, sounding shaken.

"Call Augusta. Both of you get down to the shore. Stay away from the fire. Try not to let yourselves be seen or heard. If I don't show in five get moving."

"Got it."

Dave scanned the area around him. He had to find Jerry—fast.

"You heard him," Penny whispered.

"Yeah. I'm tying my boot." Jillian fumbled with the laces in the dark.

Penny spoke into her radio. "We have a shot fired by an unknown shooter near the camp," she told the officer at headquarters two hundred miles away.

"Stay in contact. I'll put the backup team in motion now. Call if not needed."

"I copy. We may need to go silent for a while."

"Check in within ten minutes."

Penny signed off and made some rummaging noises in the darkness.

"I'm ready," Jillian whispered.

"Let me go out first. Keep low and look ahead for cover."

"Are we safer in the open?" Jillian's heart thundered as she rose and felt for Penny. Her hand grasped a fleecy sleeve.

"We're sitting ducks in here." Penny edged to the tent flap and stood still for several seconds before she cautiously unzipped it halfway.

Jillian waited behind her, tense and shivering.

"Okay," Penny whispered over her shoulder. "Let me get behind the picnic table. If everything's quiet, follow me." She ducked out of the tent.

Jillian crouched at the flap and peered outside. The moon shone over the lake between wispy clouds. After Penny's footsteps ceased, all was still. Jillian sucked in a breath and dashed out of the tent. She bumped the edge of the picnic table bench and fell headlong next to Penny.

"You okay?" Penny laid one hand on her shoulder.

Jillian rolled over and looked up at her. "Yeah." She'd probably have a beauty of a bruise on her shin tomorrow. "Do we know where Dave is?"

"No." Penny raised herself to look over the top of the table. Jillian lay still, trying to calm her heart and the sound of her breathing. After a long minute, Penny whispered, "Our next cover is that stunted tree where we hung our dish towels."

Jillian looked toward it. "All right. You first?"

"Yeah. Get ready, but stay here until you're sure I'm safe behind the tree."

Penny took off, a dark shadow in the moonlight. Jillian watched her shape meld with that of the little pine. She held her breath and waited, sending up a prayer. The lake was choppier than it had been earlier. If they had to flee the camp tonight, they'd have a wild ride.

She pushed up off the ground and sprinted for Penny's hiding place.

"Good job," Penny whispered, pulling her in behind the tree.

After two more moves, they had only one more run left to the canoe.

"When I get there, I'll drop on this side of it," Penny told her. "Wait a good minute. When you come, jump right over me and lie down in the bottom of the canoe."

Jillian gulped. "Got it."

Penny started to rise, then froze. Jillian looked beyond her and saw a dark form racing from the trees on the other side of the beach to the canoe.

TWENTY

Jillian grabbed Penny's wrist. "Did you see that?"

"Yeah." Penny eased back down behind the boulder that sheltered them. Jillian peered into the dimness. A man's form rose just beyond the canoe. He raised an arm as though beckoning to them.

"It's Dave." Relief washed over Jillian. She wanted to leave the rock and dash into his arms.

"Okay, this is good and bad. We now know where Dave is, but if Jerry was okay he'd come straight to us. You go first, and I'll cover you while you run. Keep low and jump into the canoe."

"Right."

Penny put a hand on her back. "One, two, three."

Jillian took off running. As she neared the canoe, she heard only the waves, but Dave knelt beyond the craft, aiming his pistol toward the tents. She dashed across the gravel strip and grabbed the gunwale, rolling headfirst into the canoe. The thump of her landing could probably be heard all the way down the lake. She lay panting in the bottom, staring up at a cloud oozing across the Little Dipper.

"You okay?" Dave asked.

"So far."

"Here comes Penny. Keep down."

Jillian lay still and listened to Penny's crunching footsteps. The canoe shuddered as she careened into the side and crouched, panting.

"Where is he?" Penny asked.

"Jerry or the shooter?"

"Either one," Penny said.

Dave was silent for several seconds. Jillian stirred and raised her head until she could see his profile, still wary as he covered the shadowy camp with his weapon.

"Jerry's dead."

Penny swore.

A sick feeling settled in Jillian's stomach. She swallowed back bile and waited for Dave to speak again.

"He was shot fifty feet behind your tent."

"And the shooter?" Penny asked.

"I heard something, but I couldn't get close. I think we should pull out."

"We'll make good targets out on the water."

"I know. But it's just the three of us. We can't stand him off all night. And if there's more than one . . ."

"What if he's waiting down the shore in the trees?"

Dave hauled in a deep breath. "I'm open to suggestions."

Penny was silent.

Jillian cleared her throat. "Dave's right. We can't stay here. If we could get to the warden camp—"

"Dispatch has sent out backup," Penny said. "They could be almost to the cottage by now."

Dave kept watching the campsite. "But will they be able to get up here in the dark?"

"Do you think they'd send a helicopter?" Penny asked.

"I don't know. It would take a while to get one."

Jillian bowed her head.

"If we head out toward the opposite shore, maybe we can get out of range," Penny suggested.

"Not if the shooter's got a rifle, but . . . yeah, that's probably our best bet." Dave looked down at Jillian and their gazes locked. "We will do everything we can to get you out of this, Jillian."

"I know."

"Do we have lifejackets?" he asked.

"There's only one in here."

"I put the others in the tent earlier," Penny said.

Dave nodded. "Okay. Jillian, get that jacket on. Penny, on my count, get in the canoe."

"We should shove off first. It's too far up on the beach."

Dave looked toward the camp. "You get in and—"

"No, it will be too heavy for you then."

Jillian quickly pulled on the lifejacket and fastened it. After a moment's silence, Dave said grimly, "Jillian, curl up in the bow."

As she huddled down in the front end of the canoe, another gunshot rang out. She rolled into a ball and wrapped her arms around her head, wishing the lifejacket were a bulletproof vest. Several shots were fired in quick succession, and the canoe lurched sideways. She felt it settle as more weight was added, then a shove freed them from the shore and they floated on the waves. Water splashed on her and the canoe rocked so violently she gasped and opened her eyes. Dave tumbled into the canoe and groped for a paddle.

"Can you help?" he yelled.

"Yes." Jillian unfolded herself and took the end of the paddle he held out.

"Stay as low as you can. Penny's hit."

Adrenaline surged through Jillian. Penny lay still on the floor of the canoe. Dave sat far too tall in the stern as he began to stroke, bringing the craft around and aiming it away from the beach, toward the stream at the lower end of the lake.

Jillian dug her paddle into the water. The waves buffeted them, hitting the canoe nearly broadside. She prayed in spurts. *God, help us! Help Penny. Let us live.*

From the shore, she heard the faint report of another gunshot.

After paddling frantically for twenty agonizing minutes, Dave slackened his pace and gulped air. Jillian looked back at him and he held up a hand. She laid her paddle across the gunwales and rested, breathing in deep gasps.

Dave wished they were farther down the lake. But Jillian had held her own, and they seemed to be safe for the moment. Unless more assassins waited along the shore. He'd followed Penny's advice and turned them out toward the middle of the lake. The most dangerous part of their journey would be the run down the stream.

He pushed the call button on his radio. The dispatcher answered immediately.

"We've had more shots fired. One officer wounded. We're evacuating by water."

"What about Bronte?"

"Safe so far."

Jillian's eyes widened and he would have burst out laughing if they weren't in danger. Later he'd have to explain about the code name.

"Do you think you can check on Penny?" he called to Jillian.

She shipped her paddle and scrambled to the middle of the canoe. "Penny, do you hear me?"

She moaned and shuddered.

"She's alive," Jillian said. Her eyes were huge in the moonlight. "Thank God."

Dave exhaled. "Yeah. Look, I hope we're going to get out of this . . . How deep is your faith, Jillian?"

"Bone deep. No matter what happens, I'll be all right."

He could tell she meant it. She trusted God to take care of her, not Dave Hutchins. That was as it should be. "I want you to take this." He reached under his jacket and pulled a handgun from his belt. "It's Jerry's gun."

She stared at him, then slowly reached for it.

"Here's the safety."

She nodded. "It's like Brendon's pistol."

"Good. You know how to use it."

"Yes." She unzipped a pocket at the side of her sweatshirt, shoved the gun inside and zipped it again.

"Great." Dave picked his paddle.

"Her pulse is strong," Jillian called a moment later.

Dave nodded and concentrated on his paddling rhythm. He heard Jillian speaking to Penny, but he wasn't sure if she responded.

As he put all his strength into paddling, he realized that if they survived, he couldn't go back to the way things were. Everything was different now, he thought. No matter what happened with his job, he and Jillian had to be together.

He paddled on, seeing and hearing nothing out of the ordinary. After a long time, he felt the current pulling them toward the outlet stream. The rough water would make the downriver ride dangerous. A large rock stuck up out of the water close beside them, and he used his paddle to push them away from it.

"Jillian!"

Her head jerked up.

"I need you to steer."

She climbed onto the thwart in the bow, took the paddle she'd stowed, and leaned forward, watching for rocks as she stroked.

They moved with the current now, into the rushing stream. Dave back-paddled, trying to slow their headlong pace. A tiny flash of fire caught his eye on shore and he heard the hint of a *boom* over the loud, swirling water.

"Get down!"

She looked back at him. The bow slammed into a rock and the canoe rolled. Dave dove forward for Jillian as they plunged into the icy water.

Jillian surfaced, choking on frigid water. Her body slammed against a rock. The padded life-jacket protected her some, but the current pulled at her clothing, and her feet felt clumsy inside her hiking boots. She clawed at the rock, trying to keep her position on its upstream side. The water was deeper than she'd imagined.

Something hit her in the back, and the air rushed out of her lungs. She turned and saw Penny, half-submerged and not fighting the stream. Jillian reached out and grabbed her sleeve. Penny's weight and the water pulled against her, but she found purchase on the rock and held on.

In the nightmare of cold, roaring water, she heard her name.

"Here!" She struggled to better her hold on Penny, and hiked the detective's limp body up against the side of the rock. With Penny's head out of the water, Jillian indulged in a few deep breaths. She wriggled around until her arm clutched Penny firmly across her chest. She clenched a handful of the woman's fleece pullover, determined not to let go.

Her feet, braced against the submerged rock, slipped again. She tried to hold on to the rough surface above water, but her free hand groped thin air. As the water tore her away from the rock, Penny plunged again beneath the surface. Jillian held on, kicking with all her might. The lifejacket couldn't support them both. She sank deeper, knowing that she couldn't let go of Penny.

No way could Dave right the canoe alone. He clung to the side of the nearly submerged craft as it sluggishly moved downstream. The stern got caught on a rock, and he swung around with the slender boat, until the bow caught on another rock and lodged there. For the moment at least, the canoe held on the obstacles, and the water rushed around and over it. A paddle drifted past, and Dave lunged for it.

He pushed himself along the side of the canoe. Suddenly he found he could stand up. Though the current pulled relentlessly at his frame, he could stand against it. He staggered to a rock and hauled himself onto it, shivering all over.

"Jillian!" He looked downstream and saw her, just yards away, clinging to a boulder midstream and holding Penny's head above the surface. As he watched, she lost her grip, struggled, then swung into the current. Both women disappeared beneath the water.

Dave leaped off the rock into the numbing water. Using the paddle to steady himself, he lumbered toward them.

Jillian managed to slow her passage by throwing herself against every obstacle she encountered. Against all odds, she held on to Penny. Dave's lungs burned as he inched closer to them. When he finally came within six feet of Jillian, he called her name again.

She turned her head, startled, and he shoved the canoe paddle toward her. She grabbed the end with one hand, and Dave waded to her. He fell against her, pinning her and Penny against a rock.

He caught his breath. "I'll take Penny. Can you make it to shore?"

"I don't know," Jillian said, close to his ear.

Dave looked around. They were closer to the north shore, and he was glad. The last shot had come from the south side. But the stream wasn't that wide. Anyone with a rifle could pick them off from either bank.

"Come on. If you can't make it, wait for me. I'll come back. Use the paddle if it helps you. If not, let it go."

"Can we get the canoe?"

He looked upstream. "I don't think so. It's too far back there, and I'm not sure we could right it."

"And we shouldn't go back that way anyway."

He nodded.

"Go," she said.

He put his arms around Penny's rib cage and hoisted her in a fireman's carry. Slowly he felt his way, one precarious step at a time, through the roiling water. He didn't dare look back. If Jillian tried to follow but lost her footing . . . *Lord, I can't bear to lose her now.* Guilt pummeled him. He'd come to protect Jillian, but he was leaving her in peril to rescue Penny.

He staggered to the bank and lowered Penny onto the shore. She groaned and her eyes flickered.

"Penny, I'm going to help Jillian. I'll be back." Dave turned away and pulled up short. Jillian was only a yard behind him, pushing against the water, using the paddle to propel herself toward him. He leaned toward her, holding out both arms. She grabbed one hand, and he pulled her in.

"Thank God!" He held her against him for only an instant. "Come on. Get out of the water. Up you go."

With fading strength, he boosted her up beside Penny, then crawled out and lay in the weeds, gasping.

After a minute, Jillian said, "He's out there."

Dave sat up slowly, looking toward the stream. "Can you walk?"

"I think so. But Penny—"

"I'll carry her. Where's her wound?"

The moon broke through the clouds, and Jillian's eyes glistened in its light. "Her abdomen. She needs help fast, Dave."

"Can't help it. We'll have to walk."

"But it's two miles down the river to the other lake. And if we have to walk all the way around the lake . . ."

It would take a healthy man hours to make that walk through unbroken forest, following the stream and then the lakeshore. He saw no other solution. "Pray," he said.

He rolled to his knees and tried to lift Penny gently, but she let out a groan.

"I'm sorry, Penny." He eased her onto his shoulder and looked at Jillian. "Stay close."

He staggered through the woods, keeping the stream as close to his left as he could, and trying to avoid roots and rocks. With only sporadic moonlight through the foliage, the going was slow. After ten minutes, he stopped and lowered Penny carefully to the ground.

"Sit," he told Jillian. She shivered uncontrollably.

"Maybe I should go first." She sank down beside Penny. "At least if I tripped over something, you'd know it was there and not fall with Penny."

Dave took three deep breaths before he trusted himself to answer. "The truth is, I don't know how far I can carry her. We're all soaking wet."

"Does your radio still work?"

He fumbled with it in the darkness. "Afraid not." He tried Penny's with no better results.

Penny lifted one hand and croaked, "Leave me."

Dave knelt beside her and took her icy hand. "We can't do that."

"Yes, you can. I'll be the decoy. Put me on the riverbank. If I see them, I'll flag them down to come and get me. Maybe they'll think I'm Jillian."

"Forget it," Jillian said. "Any fool can see you're not a blonde."

Even Penny cracked a smile. "You can come back for me." Her hoarse voice caught. "Go.

Send help for me. I'll be okay. I've got my gun."

"Will it still fire, even though it's wet?" Jillian asked.

"It should," Dave said, "unless it's full of river muck."

"So leave me," Penny said again.

Dave scowled at her. "Just because it's the end of May doesn't make you immune to hypothermia. Besides, you're bleeding."

"I know it. It hurts like crazy."

"We're not leaving you," Jillian said.

Penny grasped her sleeve. "Look, I've got to tell you something. A confession, sort of."

Jillian's eyes glistened, anticipating what Penny was about to say. "Don't worry about that."

"I have to. I'm the one who told the boss you were seeing Dave. And I leaked it to the radio station."

Dave stood and edged toward the water, staying beneath the trees. He was furious with Penny, but now was not the time. He studied the stream and the terrain. How many were out there, and where?

"I think we may be halfway down to the landing at the lower lake. I can carry you that far, Penny," Dave said.

"Maybe I could run from there to the warden camp to meet the backup team, and you could stay with her," Jillian said.

Dave shook his head. "I can't let you go off alone."

She sighed. "Okay. We might as well move, though. If we stay here, we'll either get bush-whacked or freeze to death."

"Hold me up," Penny said. "Maybe I can walk."

Dave pulled her to her feet. She leaned heavily against him, then crumpled to her knees.

"I'm sorry," she sobbed.

Dave said nothing, lifting her in his arms. Jillian set off, parallel to the stream.

Jillian trudged onward, running on sheer will-power and prayer. Thanks to Dave's waterproof watch, they could check the time. It was after four in the morning when they reached the mouth of the stream. She could see the broad expanse of the lake ahead, and she gave a little whoop as she burst from the underbrush onto the shore.

Dave followed her and lowered Penny again, on a sandy spot close to a large boulder.

"Can we rest here until daylight?" Jillian felt wearier than she could ever remember feeling. If only they could light a fire.

Dave sat down with a thud. "We shouldn't. It's too open here."

Jillian sat and leaned over to look at Penny. "I think she's unconscious."

Dave felt for Penny's pulse at her throat.

259

"Look, I could head for the camp now." Jillian watched his face anxiously.

"No. I told you. Besides—look how far it is."

She looked across the lake. It was much larger than the one where they'd camped.

"Hey, I can see the other shore. That means the sun will rise soon."

Dave looked at his watch again. "Four-twenty. The backup should be there."

Jillian stood and squinted at the dark water. The small waves looked much friendlier than those they'd battled a few hours ago. She peered again toward the far tip of the lake. "How far is it by land?"

"Four or five miles, maybe. Rough miles."

She looked down at Penny's inert form. "Do you think she'll make it?"

Dave didn't answer.

Jillian turned back to the lake. "Hey."

"What?" Dave looked up.

"I see something."

"Get down."

"No, it's way down there." She pointed down the lake. "I think it's a boat."

Dave stumbled to his feet and stood beside her. "Where?"

"There. See it? I wish we had the binoculars."

"You and me both." He stared for a long moment, and she held her breath, watching him.

Dave let out a chuckle. "It's a warden's boat.

They're probably towing a canoe so they can paddle upstream to us."

Jillian wanted to yell and dance and wave her soggy sweatshirt, but the thought of the assassin that had stalked them kept her still.

"We're on the wrong side of the inlet." Dave pointed to a large rock that jutted into the water. "You stay here out of sight. I'll get up there and flag them down."

Jillian sat down, noting that Penny's bluish lips trembled. If only they had a blanket. The officers coming would bring something dry.

A sudden noise in the woods startled her. She whipped her head around. Only a few yards away, a man crept stealthily between the trees. He carried a rifle with a scope on it. She shrank against the rock that sheltered her and Penny. The man wasn't looking her way. He was focused on Dave.

She swallowed back the scream that nearly choked her. If she yelled to save Dave, the man would kill her. After all, that was what he had come for.

Dave had reached the rock by the water and climbed up it. He pulled off his wet jacket and swung it over his head. "Hey!"

Jillian saw the gunman halt and look down the lake. He had advanced beyond where she and Penny hid—he wouldn't see them unless he turned around. Jillian reached for her pocket with trembling hands and fumbled with the zipper.

Her cold fingers didn't want to cooperate. Grasping the pistol with both hands, she raised it and leaned against the rock. At almost the same time, the man with the rifle put the stock to his shoulder and sighted in on Dave.

Jillian pulled the trigger.

Too late, she saw the second man step out of the woods, swinging his rifle to his shoulder, taking aim at her.

TWENTY-ONE

Two reports echoed over the water almost at once as Jillian dove for the dirt. She lay low, sheltering Penny's head. Distant yells told her the men in the boat were close to shore. Footsteps scrabbled over the rocks. Her heart thudded and she pulled the pistol up before her, expecting a killer to round the rock.

"Jillian!"

Her breath whooshed out of her. She let the gun fall and jumped into Dave's arms.

"It's okay." He held her close.

"There were two of them."

"I know. When you fired, I turned around in time to take down the second gunman. You're safe now."

The boat nudged in to shore, and two uniformed men leaped over the side, but Dave stayed with her, holding her head against his chest and stroking her hair. Jillian collapsed against him with a sob. "Penny?"

"It's okay," Dave said. "We're all going to make it." He bent his head and kissed her cheek, where the chip of granite had grazed her in January. "You saved my life."

She eased away from his embrace. One officer

had reached Penny and knelt beside her. The other rushed toward the fallen man who had tried to kill her. Dave tightened his hold around her waist and moved her down the shore, toward the boat. At the edge of the water, he pulled her into his arms again. Jillian clung to him, wanting never to be separated from him again, and they waited in silence.

When they moored at the warden camp's dock, an ambulance, two more state troopers and a game warden were waiting.

Dave helped Jillian out of the boat, and the four troopers who had come across the lake for them lifted Penny out and onto the EMTs' stretcher.

"Go inside and find some dry clothes," Dave told Jillian. "As soon as they've loaded Penny and the wounded man in the ambulance, I'll make a fire in that woodstove."

Jillian wore a jacket one of the troopers had loaned her in the boat. In the cabin, she found nothing to put on, other than blankets and one ragged hunter-orange vest.

She huddled in a wool blanket and managed to start the fire herself. By the time Dave entered, the fire was roaring. She handed him another blanket, and he draped it over his shoulders.

"How's Penny?" she asked.

Dave shrugged. "Hard to say. She was conscious

when they put the IV in. They took the wounded man, too. Half a dozen men have headed up the lake. They'll bring in the other gunman."

"They'll have to take a canoe up to our camp to get Jerry, won't they?"

"I think there's enough space to land a helicopter near the tents. They've got one coming from the Bangor National Guard station."

She nodded. Engine noises outside the cabin were followed by doors slamming and loud voices.

"Could be some media coming," Dave said.

"Way up here?"

"You're a hot story."

She swallowed hard and looked down at her clothing. "Wonderful."

"Hey, before we're inundated . . ." He looked into her eyes, and her stomach fluttered.

"Yeah?"

"I need to tell you something. I've been thinking—"

The door burst open.

"Jill! Are you all right?"

Jillian spun to face the whirlwind of Naomi and her mother. Naomi threw her arms around Jillian's neck and buried her face in her shoulder, sobbing. Jillian patted her back gently and looked at her mother.

"Thank God," Vera said. "My dear, you look splendid."

Jillian laughed and tugged at Naomi's clinging arms. "Come on, Naomi. I'm okay."

Naomi pulled away, wiping her blotchy face with the backs of her hands. "I'm so sorry, Jill. I have to tell you. This is all my fault."

Dave frowned at Naomi and set a straight chair out from the table.

"Sit, Miss Plante."

Naomi looked back toward the other room, where Jillian and her mother stood by the stove in a hug.

"Start at the beginning. Why is this your fault?"

Andrew Browne straddled one of the other chairs and laid a notebook on the table. Dave was glad he'd arrived in the first wave of reinforcements. He didn't think his fingers had thawed enough yet to hold a pen.

"I knew where you were going this weekend, and I mentioned it to a friend. I had no idea it would lead to this. Do you think—"

"Who?" Dave bent toward her and stared.

Naomi gulped. "Jack Kendall. I didn't tell anyone else."

"Did you know who he was?"

"What do you mean? He's Jack."

Dave studied her for a moment. "Did he ask you to make him a copy of the governor's schedule, and to browse her computer?"

Naomi stared at him for a moment, her face

stricken, then lowered her face into her hands. "He said . . . he wanted to meet Jillian."

"You could have introduced them."

"He couldn't come to Blaine House when I asked him to, so he wanted to know where she'd be next week, in case we could arrange it. I didn't see any harm in it." Tears streaked Naomi's face.

Dave sat down opposite her. "Tell me every time you talked to him, what he asked you to do for him, and what information you gave him. But first, tell me how you knew where we'd be on this trip."

An hour later, Carl Millbridge burst into the cabin wearing a harried expression. He spotted Jillian and strode toward her. By now she had on jeans and a Red Sox sweatshirt. Dave had requested dry clothing by radio, and one of the troopers responding to the call for backup had delivered.

"Governor, are you all right?" Millbridge asked.

"I'm fine, Detective. You didn't need to come all the way up here."

Millbridge straightened his shoulders. "I'm taking charge of the investigation."

"What about Detective Hutchins?"

"I'm told he needs medical attention."

"I'm fine," Dave growled from the kitchen doorway.

"I understand you have a prisoner."

Dave looked chagrined. "Yeah. She's in the kitchen."

Jillian stared at him. Millbridge entered the kitchen, and she heard him say, "Is this the prisoner?"

"That's right," Andrew replied.

Jillian crossed to Dave, looking into his troubled brown eyes. "You have to arrest her?"

Dave nodded. "The man you shot was Jack Kendall."

Jillian felt light-headed. Her mother stepped up beside her and slid her arm around her waist.

"Come sit down, dear."

She walked woodenly to the sofa, and her mother sat beside her. Dave pulled a chair over and sat facing her.

"Naomi didn't mean me any harm," Jillian insisted.

"You're right. She told Kendall where you'd be out of innocence, or maybe out of pride, to prove she knew your business."

"But Naomi didn't know."

Dave sighed. "It seems she did."

"How could she have? I didn't even know until we were partway here."

"She did some snooping in Ryan's pockets the night before we left."

Jillian's jaw dropped. "She picked his pockets?"

"He hung his jacket in the security office at

the Blaine House. While he made his rounds, she snooped and got lucky. Ryan had your fishing license and the fire permits with the locations on them in his jacket."

Vera patted her shoulder. "I'm so sorry, dear."

A pain started deep in Jillian's stomach. "Who was the other man? Tanger? They wouldn't release him without telling us."

Dave shook his head. "No. But we'll find out." He leaned toward her and took her hands in his. "Jack Kendall is still alive."

She caught her breath. "I'm glad. I mean—"

He nodded. "I'm glad, too. You didn't kill him. It may take some time to put it all together, but we hope Kendall will survive and tell us exactly what was on his mind."

"But Naomi didn't know he was coming up here?"

"She says she didn't, and I believe her. They went out Saturday night, but he told her he was busy on Sunday. That's when he came up here."

"With a friend."

"It seems that way."

"But the parking garage? The inauguration day shooting? And Wesley Stevenson. How does it all fit together?"

"There's still a lot we don't know."

"Can you take us home, David?" Vera said gently. "My daughter needs to rest."

"Sure, Mrs. Clark."

"No." Jillian reached out to him. "Take me to the hospital where they took Penny. I need to see her."

Dave eyed her keenly, then turned to Vera. "That all right with you, ma'am?"

Vera nodded curtly. "We'll get a doctor to look Jillian over while we're at it."

"Mom, I'm okay."

Dave smiled for the first time in what seemed like a long, long time. "Mrs. Clark, I like the way you think."

They dropped Vera off at her home at ten that evening.

"Are you sure you won't stay here tonight, honey?" she asked Jillian before she got out of the vehicle.

"No, thanks, Mom. I need to go to my office tomorrow and hold a press conference so everyone knows I'm okay."

"What will you say?"

Jillian sighed. "Lettie will write up something for me."

Dave saw Vera into the house, then got back in the driver's seat. He put the key in the ignition and then changed his mind, taking it out and turning to her. "Jillian, this may not be a good time, but there are things I need to say. Things that have been on my mind for some time now. And after everything we've just been through, I don't think I can keep them to myself anymore."

She looked at him expectantly. "You can say anything to me, Dave. I mean that."

He took a deep breath, intending to explain how he fell for her, and how torturous it was for him not to be able to see her after Penny reported him, but what came out of his mouth was, "I love you."

She caught her breath. "Oh, Dave. I . . ."

"You don't have to say anything, Jillian. I know this might be strange for you to hear. But I was afraid I'd lose you last night, and I realized that I don't want a world without you."

Tears welled in her eyes, and she felt a prickly lump in her throat. "Dave, I love you, too."

Dave could hardly believe his ears. He leaned over and caressed her cheek. "I'll do whatever it takes to be with you, Jillian." His lips met hers, and he kissed the lovely governor of Maine as he'd wanted to for so long.

EPILOGUE

Colonel Gideon Smith sat across from Jillian in her statehouse office and opened a folder he carried. "We're putting this thing together, little by little. Jack Kendall is conscious, and our officers interviewed him this morning."

"And?"

"He claims he acted without his father's knowledge. His father said as much before, but we wanted to hear it from Kendall."

"But he had two of his father's old cronies helping him."

"Yes." Smith looked down at the papers in the folder. "Wesley Stevenson and the man who accompanied Kendall to the lake on Sunday—Daryl Leigh. Both worked for Roderick Tanger in the past."

"So why were they helping Tanger's son try to kill me?"

Smith looked at her with sympathy. "Jack Kendall's mother told us, and he admitted himself this morning, that he blamed you for putting his father in prison. Jack was only fourteen at the time. In his mind, you're the one who kept his father from being part of his life."

Jillian stared at him. "That's ridiculous. His

parents were divorced before the trial."

"Yes, they were. But the boy wanted to live with his father. After Tanger was convicted of several felonies, full custody went to the mother. And don't forget, Tanger swore revenge on you in the courtroom for allegedly bungling his defense."

"I know," Jillian said drily. "I was there."

"The boy heard about it. He was at an impressionable age, and he got a stepfather he didn't care for. His mother made him take his stepfather's name. Kendall had a lot of anger and resentment, and he focused it on you."

Jillian released a breath. "But these two thugs. How did he connect with them?"

Smith frowned. "When the young man learned you'd been elected governor of Maine, he came here from Massachusetts and looked up some of the men who had worked for his father. Kendall paid them—we're still digging to find out where he got the money. First he hired Stevenson to shoot you. Then Kendall sniffed out Leigh. He decided to wait for precisely the right opportunity this time. And he formed a liaison with a close friend of yours—Naomi Plante."

Jillian held up a hand in protest. "But Colonel, Naomi met him through a young man she dated a couple of times—the cousin of Beth, one of our kitchen staff at Blaine House."

"Yes. We believe that young man, Sean Broule, had nothing to do with this. He says Kendall showed up at the club where he took Miss Plante one night and insisted on an introduction. Broule knew him only slightly, and we now know that was another machination of Kendall's. During his time in Augusta, trying to find a way to access you, Jack Kendall learned Broule's cousin worked at the mansion and struck up an acquaintance. At first he hoped to gain influence with Beth, but then he found that Sean was dating your personal assistant. So he followed Broule and Miss Plante that evening. I understand from Miss Plante that it took him several weeks to convince her to go out with him."

"Yes." Jillian felt tears fill her eyes as she recalled her conversations with Naomi.

"He was a good ten years younger than her," Smith said. "I expect she found it exciting that a handsome twenty-four-year-old found her attractive."

"He didn't really care about her, did he?"

"I'm afraid not. He used her to determine the perfect opportunity to attack you and finish the job."

"The camping trip," Jillian said.

"Yes. When you invited Miss Plante on the trip, she'd already promised a date with him. She says she was the one who had the idea of finding out your destination, to impress him, but I wonder if Kendall didn't subtly suggest it. It was careless of Mills to leave the information where it could be accessed."

"I hope Ryan won't be disciplined."

Smith sighed. "His father passed away yesterday, and he's taking the rest of the week off. I'll address that issue when he comes back on duty."

"And what about Daryl Leigh, the man who accompanied Kendall to the lake?" she asked.

"Kendall said he planned originally for Leigh to follow you to the campsite and shoot you there. But when he discovered how remote the site was, he told Leigh he would go with him."

Jillian forced herself to remember the nightmare of Sunday night. "I don't know which of them killed Jerry Knott, or who shot Penny, but in the end, it was Jack Kendall who took the first shot at the lake. I'll testify against him. He may be able to blame Leigh for the other shootings, but he had Dave Hutchins in his sights."

"So I'm told. Detective Hutchins says Kendall would have killed him for certain if you hadn't fired first."

"Yes." Jillian frowned, remembering the older man turning his weapon toward her after she'd shot Jack Kendall. Dave's bullet had killed him instantly. She shuddered. "I'm glad it's over."

"As we all are." Smith arched an eyebrow at her. "The district attorney will decide whether or not to bring charges against Miss Plante."

"She didn't mean to hurt me. I'm sure of it."

"Nevertheless, we'll have to ban her from

Blaine House." Smith closed his folder. "That's it for now. My department will keep you informed as we learn more."

"There's one more thing we need to discuss, Colonel." Jillian sat straighter and looked steadily into his steely eyes.

"Oh? Have I overlooked something, ma'am?"

"I intend to marry one of your officers."

Smith's mouth worked for a few seconds before he spoke. "I hardly know what to say. Is the officer in question by any chance Detective Hutchins?"

"That's correct. I respect you, sir, and I wanted you to have time to consider what changes will be made. Detective Hutchins has told me he's willing to accept a different position within the state police department if that will be best for the administration."

He cleared his throat. "I know that Hutchins is a competent officer. His lieutenant thinks highly of him. He did an excellent job of getting you and Detective Thurlow home alive."

"Yes, he did." Jillian held his gaze.

"But you must understand, ma'am, that we have to avoid further scandal."

"I do." She rose, walked over to the window, looked out for a moment, then faced him. "You and I have worked well together for the last five months. I want to continue our good relationship."

"As do I."

"Then please let David Hutchins go back to regular duty as a state police detective outside the EPU, without any publicity."

He pursed his lips and nodded. "We can do that."

"Thank you."

"Might I suggest, ma'am, that as a matter of discretion, you wait at least three months before announcing an engagement? Allow the memory of this weekend to mellow a little, and let past rumors die. Get past the hearings on Monday's shootings."

Jillian's knees began to tremble slightly, and she sat down. Again Dave would have to undergo the requisite investigation of an officer who had shot a suspect. As to her own role in the drama, she supposed she was the first governor to shoot a man while in office. The thought made her shudder.

"Are you all right, ma'am?"

"Yes. Colonel, I assure you that we will practice the utmost discretion."

He eyed her keenly. "Yes, ma'am, I believe you will."

She shook his hand and watched him leave, then sank back into her chair. She stared down at her hands for a moment. Slowly, she removed her wedding ring from her left hand and placed it in a drawer. Tears stung her eyes. She inhaled deeply and firmly shut the drawer.

• • •

Dave bounded up the marble stairs at five o'clock. It felt great to be in the statehouse again, especially for the purpose of escorting Jillian home from her office. The man on guard in the outer office grinned at him and motioned for him to come over.

"Hey, Hutchins, just so you know—the colonel's inside with the governor."

"Ah. Thanks."

Lettie smiled at Dave as she rose from her desk. "I'm sure it will just be a few minutes, Detective. Would you like to sit over here?"

"Thank you, ma'am." Dave sat and watched Lettie tidy her desk.

"How is Detective Thurlow doing?" Lettie asked.

"Much better," Dave said.

When the door to the inner office opened, he jumped up. Colonel Smith came out and stopped in front of him. Dave was aware of Lettie and the security guard watching.

Smith gave a short cough. "Hutchins. My office, eight tomorrow morning."

"Yes, sir."

The colonel nodded crisply and strode out.

When he had left the room, Dave exhaled and turned toward the door.

"Go right in, Detective," Lettie said.

Jillian stood when he entered, closing the door

softly behind him. They faced each other, not moving.

"He's called me to his office tomorrow," Dave said.

"I'm sure he only wants to congratulate you privately and settle the details of your transfer."

"You asked him?"

"Yes. He agreed."

"I'll keep my rank?"

"Absolutely."

Dave grinned. He took two strides, closing the gap between them, and reached for her hands. She smiled up at him.

"Jillian, I love you more than I can tell you. Will you—"

She reached up and laid her index finger across his lips, but her eyes glittered. "We have to keep it a secret over the summer."

Dave threw back his head and laughed. "Of course we do."

"Do you mind terribly? The colonel suggested we wait three months. But he'll get you transferred at once, so we can see each other."

"Three months? That's nothing, compared to the rest of our lives. I think that's reasonable."

"Do you, Detective?"

"I do, Governor."

He grinned at her as he pulled her close and kissed her, knowing she was finally safe. And he intended to keep it that way.

Dear Reader,

This story brewed in the back of my mind for a long time. Writing about a public figure, albeit a fictional one, seemed daunting. Maine has never yet had a female governor, and such a situation might change things at the Blaine House and within the Executive Protection Unit. Visitors who tour the EPU are somewhat guarded by the public safety department for understandable reasons. I asked lots of questions, learned what I could, and guessed at the rest. I accept responsibility for any errors in these pages.

The heart of this story does not lie in politics, the technical details of how the governor of Maine lives or how the unit protects her. The heart of this story is duty and honor. Jillian and Dave are determined to fulfill their responsibilities honorably, even if that means denying love. This challenge might face anyone in any job, but the fact that they are constantly watched by the public—and the person who wants Jillian dead—makes their struggle more painful.

People in public service often must sacrifice aspects of their personal lives. In this story, two people who love each other must maintain a distance. Other conflicts wear on them—Jillian's fear and grief; Dave's frustration and suffering from false accusations. But they both have a sense of honor that some might consider old-fashioned. Both believe in upholding the law and keeping promises, no matter what. Their faith in God and His love for them enables them to do that.

I hope you enjoy Jillian and Dave's journey. You can learn more about the magnificent Blaine mansion at: www.blainehouse.org. I love to hear from readers. Come visit me at: www.susanpagedavis.com.

Susan Page Davis

QUESTIONS FOR DISCUSSION

1. After Jillian is shot at during a press conference, she reacts in fear and anger. How does she deal with these emotions? How do the people around her help her?

2. Jillian's mother has trouble dealing with her daughter's status as a public figure. How does she attempt to protect and encourage Jillian? How does she hinder Jillian in adapting to her new role?

3. Jillian remembers only the good about Brendon and sees him as more competent and intelligent than she is. She tells herself that if he had lived, he would be the governor, not her. How is this counterproductive to Jillian's growth?

4. How do Jillian's memories of her strong marriage help her? What would you tell a widowed person about moving on, versus clinging to the past?

5. Dave doesn't mind remaining behind the scenes in the EPU. He feels investigating is one of his strongest skills. Have you been

blessed with a job you love and are good at? Does it bother you if you don't get the credit for your work?

6. When Dave is accused of unprofessional behavior, he accepts the consequences. How would God have us react if we are falsely accused?

7. Both Jillian and Dave have prickly relationships with Colonel Smith. Penny admits she is not Jillian's biggest fan, but she still risks her life daily to protect Jillian. How would you reconcile duty with dislike? Have you ever had to work with someone whose personality grated on yours? How did you handle it?

8. Jillian is placed in a position of trust on many levels. How does the Blaine mansion symbolize that?

9. It's said that people either loved or hated James G. Blaine, the former owner of the governor's residence. What strong personalities have you encountered? How did you maintain your courtesy and respect for them while retaining your dignity?

10. Jillian chafes constantly at her lack of freedom. How can you go beyond the walls that enclose you? What advice could you give a shut-in? At what point would you sacrifice security for liberty?

11. Jillian feels guilty because she has not overtly witnessed to her friend Naomi. Has her outward life been enough of a testimony concerning her faith? What would you advise Jillian to do?

12. Penny and Naomi both betrayed Dave and Jillian. What consequences do you think each should face? Can you forgive someone who has hurt you out of jealousy or ambition?

Susan Page Davis

is a native of central Maine. She and her husband, Jim, have six children and five grandchildren. Susan has many years of experience as a freelancer for a daily newspaper. Her four Love Inspired Suspense books are set in central Maine. Her other books include ten historical novels, two children's books and several romantic suspense novels. She also writes cozy mysteries with her daughter, Megan. Visit Susan's Web site at www.susanpagedavis.com.

Center Point Publishing

600 Brooks Road ● PO Box 1
Thorndike ME 04986-0001 USA

(207) 568-3717

US & Canada:
1 800 929-9108

www.centerpointlargeprint.com